IN THE WEST OF TEXAS

A TOOMBS SULLIVAN ADVENTURE

BOOK SEVEN

TOM PILGRIM

For information contact: info@outlawspublishing.com
Cover Art by Michael Thomas
Cover design by Outlaws Publishing LLC
Published by Outlaws Publishing LLC
November 2024
10987654321

Chapter One

Toombs Sullivan looked down on the little town of El Paso.

That is what the whites and Mexicans called it, El Paso. To others it was the pass in whatever language they spoke. It was where you crossed the Rio Grande River and went into Mexico or came back into Texas. A lot of people came back into Texas. That is what the problem was, and that is why Toombs Sullivan had been sent there.

People had been living in that area for thousands of years.

The Spanish explorers had come there in the 1500s. By the year 1859 there were about four hundred people living there in what was becoming a town.

When Sullivan looked down on the town in 1871, he saw adobe buildings and places on the street where women and children sold fruit and vegetables and bread.

Beyond the town there were orchards and vineyards and cotton fields.

Goods came into El Paso by wagon from the Gulf of Mexico.

El Paso had become a rough town with wild living and lots of gambling where as much as $100,000.00 was lost at night.

Fort Bliss was near the town. It had been established there by order of Secretary of War Jefferson Davis on January 11, 1854. The fort was named after Lt. Col. William Wallace Smith Bliss for his gallantry during the Mexican War. It was located one mile north of the Rio Grande River. Water had to be hauled to the fort by mule team wagons every day.

Across the river from El Paso to the south-west was Mexico. To the west and north was the New Mexico territory.

There were people there other than whites, soldiers, and Mexicans. There were Apache, Comanches, and Comancheros.

There were bitter feelings amongst the Indians. Many had been forced onto reservations. Uprisings were common. It was often more than the Army could address. This had always been the reason for the existence of the Texas Rangers. It was why men like Toombs Sullivan were needed.

As Sullivan looked at the town of El Paso, he knew what his job was. He had been told, but he did not have to be told.

More and more white settlers were moving into that part of Texas, organizing more and more ranches and farms, creating more and more friction and more and more opportunities for those who did not want them there. West Texas was a powder keg. The fuse was there.

The Indians had the fire. And they had the fire-power also.

Toombs Sullivan also had the fire-power. He had the new 1870 Smith & Wesson Model 3 Revolver, .44 caliber, single action six-shooter. It fired the first big-bore metal cartridge. He now wore a belt with a holster for the first time in order to have the cartridges in that belt for quick and convenient use. He had his 1866 Winchester, .44 caliber, with a full-length barrel. It was called the Yellow Boy because of the brass housing. He carried a .41 caliber Deringer pistol tucked in his pants belt on his left side. His knife was in a case tucked in his right boot on the outside. His favorite weapon was still his Sharps single shot rifle. It was his long-distance man killer. He preferred long distance.

Most of the Texas Rangers had the same weapons Sullivan had. So did William Boyd who was with him.

The problem was the Indians had all these weapons and more.

They bought them, traded for them, stole them, and took them off of their victims. They were often better armed than the U S Army.

Into that situation, Toombs Sullivan rode in the Spring of the year 1871.

When he and his men left south Texas, he sent a telegram to Major Pendergrass.

"Mission accomplished Stop Coming back to Austin Stop

Arrive in a few days Stop Sullivan Stop"

As they headed out toward Austin, he wondered what was next.

Chapter Two

Back in Austin, Toombs Sullivan went to report to Major Pendergrass. He sat across from his desk, waiting for him to begin the conversation.

"So you took care of this General De Vega?"

"We took care of him."

"I won't ask you where it was that you took care of him."

"Good."

"But maybe you crossed the river?"

"I can't recall."

"All right. Well, Captain . . . ."

"Beg ya pardon?"

"You are now a captain. Not doing you any favors. I need you to be that and do a job I need you to do."

"Yes, Sir."

"We got a problem at El Paso."

"Problem?"

"Yep. Company M is over there. You never met Jacob Martin. He was the captain. They were jumped by some Apache. He was killed along with Sergeant Seeb Myers. The rest of the men fought them off, but the loss of their two leaders was devastating of course. You are now the captain of Company M. You need a sergeant to go with you. Ideas?"

"Boyd."

"Good. You tell him. Now, El Paso is different. You got Fort Bliss there. They have lots of problems. The Indians are only one. This place is a mix of cultures. It is not the sleepy little town it used to be. It is wide open and wild at times. Mostly Mexican for a long time. But now ya got white settlers all around and in town. Those settlers are being attacked by Apaches and Comanches and Comancheros who don't want them being there except they are glad they are there because they are sitting ducks. Lots of stuff for the Indians to take, steal, rob, and of course kill all they can.

"Lots of people moving into that area all the time. Running from the south and the so-called reconstruction which they don't like and can't live with.

"You'll need to check in at the fort. Let them know you are there. Get to know their commander, a Colonel Anthony Kicklighter.

"You will be in charge of that whole Rio Grande River area from the New Mexico Territory all the way down to, uh, God knows where, far south. To Eagle Pass and as far east as you need to go depending."

"Depending?"

"Depending on what happens to who and where they are."

"When do we leave?"

"You need some time to rest up. I'd say leave tomorrow or the next day."

"I'm fine. My horse needs a day off and some good feeding."

"The next day is fine, but here's an idea. Catch a supply convoy going there. They come through all the time. Stop, rest up, and then head out to El Paso. Slow you down a little, but you'll have plenty of water all the way and some good food. Better than you and Boyd can cook up on the way."

"Sounds like a good idea."

"Anything else? Questions?"

"No, Sir. I'll go find Boyd."

"Good luck to ya both."

"Thanks."

Sullivan left the office and walked across the street to the saloon where he knew he would find Boyd and the other Rangers. When he saw Boyd, he got his attention and motioned him over to a vacant table.

"Good to be back here," Boyd said, as he sat down where Sullivan was already seated.

"Don't get too attached, Sergeant Boyd."

"Huh? What?"

"You are now a sergeant and I am a captain, and that is where the fun ends. Pendergrass is sending us to El Paso."

"El Paso?"

"Company M over there needs a captain and a sergeant and we are them. They got ambushed by some Apache who killed their two leaders."

"Well, couldn't he promote somebody over there? Why me? Why us?"

"He didn't tell me that. He just said we are the ones. There are big problems there."

Sullivan then told Boyd about the Indians, the settlers, the mixed cultures, the growing town, and Fort Bliss.

"All right, Captain. When do we leave?"

"He would prefer tomorrow or the next day. But he said we might be better off to catch a freight convoy going there. Better food, better security too I think."

"Fine. Maybe we can catch one in a week or two."

"Afraid not. Sergeant."

Chapter Three

Three days later, as Sullivan finished up his breakfast in the hotel dining room, Boyd came walking back in, having finished a few minutes earlier.

"Well, Sir," he said, "I found us a freighter going to El Paso. He's got four wagons. Each one pulled by eight mules. Each wagon has a driver and a guard. He rides on his horse so he can scout out ahead. I told him if we could go along, we could do some of that. He seemed to like the idea. How's that?"

"Good work. When's he leavin?"

"He's pullin' out right now. I told we'd catch up on the road."

Sullivan took his coffee cup in his right hand and turned it up, draining it of the rest of his coffee.

"My gear is packed up ready to go. Yours?" he asked Boyd.

"Yep. Everthang I got."

"We'll need the mule."

"I'll go get the mule and our horses and bring'em down out front."

"Good," Sullivan replied. "I'll meet ya out there."

Almost an hour later, Sullivan and Boyd rode out of Austin headed west. It wasn't long until they caught up with the freighters. They rode to the front of the line where they found the foreman on his horse. When he saw them, he pulled off to the side, letting the wagons go on by.

"This is Captain Tooms Sullivan," Boyd said. "And this is Buck McFalls."

"McFalls, glad to meet ya."

"Me too," he answered, as he spit tobacco juice off to his right side. "Glad to have y'all along. Let's get on up ahead or we'll be eatn' dust all day."

The three of them pulled on ahead of the four wagons. When they got there, they slowed as McFalls turned to them.

"Ever been to El Paso?"

"Nope", Sullivan answered. "Been all over that part of the state along the river, but never been in the town."

"Me neither," Boyd said.

"Needless to say, we been there a lot," McFalls said. "It has changed so much since we been going there, and a lot of the change has been in these wagons we pulled in there. It was a village sort of. But it is a town now. Busy. Wild at times. But all in all, it ain't a bad place now."

"Good to know," Sullivan said.

"Texas Rangers, eh. You going there for a reason?"

"Yeah, we're taking over the company there."

"Permanently?"

"Well, yeah, I guess so. For a while. Don't know how long of course."

"The captain they had and his sergeant thought they was there permanent. But they weren't. Yep, we heard about it. Bad business. Apache. Better be careful."

"We intend to do just that."

There was not much conversation for the rest of the day.

Sullivan and Boyd continued to ride out front. McFalls was back and forth, checking on the wagons and the mules a lot.

Not long after three o'clock, McFalls pulled alongside of Sullivan and Boyd.

"They's a place up yonder where we always camp the first night. I'm goin' on ahead to check it out. See ya in a bit."

"Sure," Sullivan replied.

Thirty minutes later, they came to McFalls. His horse was tied at a creek. He was gathering firewood and placing it where it was obvious there had been many fires.

"Welcome home!" he called out. "Not many comforts here, but it'll do for one night."

"Fine by me," Sullivan replied.

He and Boyd dismounted and led their horses to the water. After the horses had enough to drink, they tied them to small trees.

They all set up camp with the drivers and guards doing most of the chores. The fires were started. Tables were taken off the wagons and set up along with everything needed for preparing the meal. Two of the drivers always cooked the food, and they were good at it. After an hour or so, the food was ready to be served. It consisted of fried beef, pan-fried potatoes, beans, and bread, along with coffee. Not much was left when the meal was over.

After eating, they all sat around the fires and talked.

Sullivan said to McFalls, "Tell me about ourself. How did you get into this hauling?"

McFalls was a tall and lean looking man of about forty years of age it appeared. He wore a big flop hat to keep the sun off. He had a short beard of blond and a little gray. His hair was long and a mixture of colors and shades. His boots reached up to his knees, obvious protection from rattlesnakes. His shirt and pants were light brown. He still wore in his holster his Colt Navy pistol from the war, and he had a large knife on his gun-belt.

"Came here to Texas after the war on a boat from New Orleans. Had nothing left up the state. Needed to be able to eat and lay my head some place. Saw a sign on a wall in Galveston about needing haulers. I grew up following a mule, driving a wagon to town to market. Sounded like a good idea at the time. I went inside and told P. J. Stephens what I just told you. I guess he liked what I said. Hired me that day. The next day I was driving a wagon to El Paso. Been doing it ever since. I outlasted all the other drivers. Lots of men signed on, did it a while, and then quit to find something they liked better. I like it fine. Stayed with it, and that is why I now lead every trip."

"Run into any trouble along the way anytime?"

"Where could I begin? Mules running away. Indians stealing mules and horses. Fightin' Indians, robbers, crooks. I didn't sign on to fight Indians, but I found it goes with the job. I like my hair and want to keep it. So I do whatever I have to do, ya know?"

"I do know," Sullivan said, with a little laugh.

"It's a long way ya know to El Paso. About six hundred miles from Austin as the crow flies, but we ain't crows and we ani't flyin'. And we can't go on no straight shot. We got to go by San Angelo, cut north a ways. Fort Concho is there ya know. Buffalo Soldiers, the Black cavalry."

"Oh, yeah, I know. I been there."

"Got some items to drop off in town and also at the fort. Good thing is we get to spend the night in a hotel stead of trying to sleep out like this. And there's the north and south Concho Rivers. Good water for the animals. So out of the way, but worth it."

"I agree."

"I'm going to sleep. The boys will guard during the night. Rest well."

"Thanks. You too."

Chapter Four

The next day, the journey continued. Though it was still the Spring, it was already hot. The men felt it and the animals felt it. They were hauling enough water to be all right until they came to another river or creek. But the dust was smothering behind the wagons. McFalls, Sullivan, and Boyd made sure they stayed out front well ahead of them.

Sullivan kept thinking about El Paso, what it was like, what the days ahead would be like, what the Rangers there would be

like. He already knew what the Comanches, Comancheros, and Mexican bandits would be like. He was less certain about the Apaches.

"What you so deep in thought about?" Boyd asked him.

"Oh, just wondering what we are gettin' into over there in El Paso."

"I reckon we'll find out soon enough."

"Yeah. That's what I'm concerned about."

"Me?" said McFalls, "all I got to do is keep these mules alive and movin'. The rest will take care of itself. Unless . . . ."

"Unless?" Sullivan asked.

"Unless we run into some bad people or mad Indians. Then if that be the case, we got trouble."

"I have had trouble before, me and Boyd, from the aforementioned bad people and mad Indians. But they weren't bad or mad when we got through with them."

"Happy huntin' ground?" McFalls asked.

"Yep. The very same."

"Let's keep it that way. I'm going on ahead a ways and take a look around."

"We'll be along."

Over an hour later, McFalls came back to the wagon train. He stopped in front of Sullivan and Boyd.

"Saw some Indian sign up ahead. Indian pony tracks from north heading south. Not too old I don't think. Mixed in were a good many shod horses. Likely they raided somebody and took their horses. Hope they don't see our dust and come circling around to see who we are. You don't never know what they gonna do."

"Me and Boyd could ride a little south of you. Go parallel to ya. See if we see anything of them. We could give you an early warning that way."

"That would shore be nice of ya. But I don't want you getting into it with them. Just be careful."

"We will. Come on Boyd."

Sullivan and Boyd pulled their horses to the left and headed south. They went about a half a mile, came to a rise, dismounted, tied their horse, and walked up it. Sullivan had his binoculars with him. He slowly scanned around to the south, west and then back east.

"What ya see?" Boyd asked.

"Nothin' yet."

"That's good."

"That is very good."

Sullivan thought a minute, as he continued looking around.

"You know what, Boyd?"

"What?"

"If those are Comanches, and they are in a horse stealing mood, and if they have seen our dust, and if they want more horses and mules, then we will never see them. Not in the daytime. They will wait until we camp tonight."

"I'm afraid you are right."

"Let's move on further west and take another look."

They walked back down to the horses, mounted up, and headed west. As they rode along, they kept their eyes open, constantly looking around, especially to their left. They saw nothing.

"Sullivan, I don't see any birds fluttering around, being scared off."

"That's a good sign."

By mid-afternoon, they decided there was no threat from the Indians. They headed toward McFalls and his wagons. They soon reached them.

"We never did see anything," Sullivan reported. "We did cross all those tracks you saw earlier. Still headed south."

"Good," McFalls replied. "Maybe we'll be all right."

"What ya got in mind for camping?"

"One of our places is not far ahead. Good water. We'll be there in a bit. You Boys stay with the wagons. I'll go ahead on and check it out."

"Sure."

McFalls went ahead of them. Sullivan and Boyd led the wagons.

An hour later, they reached the site. McFalls had a fire already.

Sullivan and Boyd dismounted as the wagons pulled into their place. McFalls looked up and spoke.

"Welcome home. If the smoke from this fire don't tell them where we are, then they just ain't interested in finding us."

"Let's hope that is the case," Sullivan responded.

"On the other hand, and there is always the other hand, another hand, they just might see this smoke, since we don't know where they are, but we can't live like we hiding from them."

"We been thinking they wouldn't come at us in the daytime, but would wait until tonight. That is if gettin' more horses and mules is what they want, and it likely is just that."

"Yep."

Soon the food was ready. It was set out on the table along with plates, forks, cups, and the coffee pot. The men sat around on stumps, large stones, and some on the ground. When they were finished eating, each man washed his plate and cup in the creek.

Sullivan walked over to McFalls who was standing by one of the wagons.

"Me and Boyd will take the first watch. We need to do our part."

"Well, you're doing that just being here and being outriders today. I thank ya."

"Glad to do it."

By then it was dark. The men settled in. Some went to sleep quickly. Others were like Sullivan and had trouble going to sleep always.

Sullivan and Boyd were relieved that it was an uneventful night.

Chapter Five

Several days later they pulled into San Angelo. The men were glad to be there for several reasons. They would be able to sleep in beds in the hotel. They could eat food either in the hotel or at one of the saloons. And there was plenty to drink in those saloons. All of this made for a nice break from the rough traveling they had done.

Sullivan and Boyd were also glad to be there for the same reasons.

However, the first order of business was to unload a few items at a couple of stores. The deliveries to Fort Concho would be made the next morning.

Sullivan and Boyd put their horses and the mule in a livery stable. They took their saddlebags and rifles with them to the hotel and checked in.

As soon as they put their belongings in their room, they went downstairs. They walked down the street to a saloon. It was late afternoon, and they were ready to eat.

"What'll you Boys have?" the waitress said, as soon as they sat down.

She was a tall woman with black hair pulled up on her head. Her lips were red. She wore a black dress up close to her neck with long sleeves. She glared at them as though she wanted an immediate reply. She had a stern expression and a demanding kind of voice.

"Oh," answered Sullivan. "What ya got?"

"We got steak or steak and gravy or chicken or chicken and gravy with beans and biscuits or biscuits and gravy."

With a puzzled expression on his face, Boyd looked over at Sullivan.

Sullivan thought for a moment then replied.

"I'll have chicken and gravy, beans, and biscuits and gravy. I'm originally from Georgia. I'm partial to gravy."

"I gathered that. What about you?" she said, as she looked down at Boyd.

"I'll have steak. No gravy. Beans. Biscuits. No gravy. I'm not from Georgia."

"Thank God," she replied. "What to drink? Both of you."

"Coffee."

"Coffee."

"Be out in a bit," she said.

When she walked away, Boyd looked back over at Sullivan.

"I was almost afraid to order anything."

"Yeah. I bet her bite is worse than her bark."

"Hope she don't put poison in our food."

"Or spit in it."

"I'd rather have the poison," Boyd said.

Twenty minutes later, she brought out their plates.

"Thanks," Sullivan said, "What's your name, if I may ask."

"Well, you did anyway. It's Henrietta DePlese."

"I'm Toombs Sullivan. This is William Boyd. We're Texas Rangers. We came in with the freight wagons this afternoon."

"Wonderful. Sorry I asked."

"But you didn't . . . ." Sullivan tried to say, as she walked away.

"Nice lady," Boyd said sarcastically.

"Let's eat."

Soon the freighters came in and walked over to the bar. They began drinking beer. Then they ordered two bottles and took them over to a couple of tables. They passed the bottles around, filling up their glasses. They downed one glass-full after another.

"Hey!" one of them yelled out. "We want food!"

The waitress walked over to them.

"What do you want?" she asked.

"What ya got, Baby?" another freighter asked loudly.

"Steak is all we have. And beans. And biscuits."

"You got any gravy for them bis . . . . cuits?"

"We don't serve gravy. You will have to go to Georgia to get gravy."

"I wish I was still in Geor . . . . Carolina instead of here."

"I wish you were also. That could be arranged."

"Can . . . . you arrange that?"

"No. But I would if I could."

Another raised his hand.

"Lady, they don't know what they're sayin'. Just bring steaks and beans and biscuits all around. No gravy please."

"Maybe we better eat up and get out of here," Boyd said.

"I think you are right. Hopefully they won't look over here and recognize us."

After the meal, Sullivan and Boyd walked outside and looked up and down the street. It was fairly busy, with people going in and out of stores.

"Let's walk down here and look in some of these stores," Sullivan said.

They came to a general store, stopped, looked inside, then entered it. They saw everything imaginable from hats to guns to coats to candy to boots to cloth to saddles to sacks of flower.

"See anything you need?" Sullivan asked.

"Nothin' I need, a lot I want. Let's get out of here."

The next morning, deliveries were made at Fort Concho. The freighters did not look very well. But they were able to do their jobs. That was what McFalls asked of them.

By nine o'clock, they were headed out to El Paso.

Chapter Six

Days later, they came near El Paso. Sullivan and Boyd were out ahead of McFalls and his wagons. They looked down on the town, its adobe buildings, some newer buildings, hotels and saloons, streets, the people they saw, the women selling fruits, vegetables, trinkets, beads.

"Well," Sullivan said, "this is our new home. For a while at least."

"Hope it ain't forever. It don't look like much."

"We'll get used to it."

"Afraid so."

Sullivan looked over at Boyd.

"Let's go find our Boys."

They rode on into town, stopping at a hotel. They tied their horses to the rail out front. They stepped up on the boardwalk, then went inside.

"Howdy," Sullivan said, to the man at the desk. "We're lookin' for some Texas Rangers."

"You don't have to look far. That'd be them rat over thar."

Sullivan and Boyd turned around and looked toward the parlor. Ten men stood up. They had heard what Sullivan asked.

"We're Rangers," one of them said.

"I'm Toombs Sullivan. This is William Boyd."

"Glad to meet ya," the young man said, as he walked toward them. "I'm Timothy Davis, Corporal. We got word y'all was comin'." He was tall and thin with a boney face, brown hair, and dark eyes. His smile revealed dimples in his cheeks. "The rest can introduce themselves."

They all stepped forward, hats in their hands. They were dressed like most Texas Rangers wearing high boots, pants tucked in, mostly light brown, shirts that were blue, red, or green, vests, kerchiefs around their necks, and gun-belts holding their pistols.

"I'm Caleb Hanson." He was very young, blond, light mustache hardly visible, medium height and weight.

"Slim Pardue." He was very slim and tall, dark skin, heavy mustache, brown hair and eyes.

"Richard English." Heavyset, not tall, dark hair and eyes.

"Cap Bridges." Tall and wiry looking, black hair, dark eyes, very thin face.

"Johnny Dickens." He was the youngest looking one, boyish face, blue eyes, light colored hair, and a ready smile.

"Billy Crowe." Appeared to be the oldest one of them, dark skin, a touch of gray hair on his temples, a noticeable scar down across his face from his left ear to his mouth.

"Charles Easom." He was the shortest among them, but looked very muscular, light hair, no facial hair.

"Eddie Canton." Medium build, heavy facial hair shadow, but only a mustache and goatee.

"Tommy Crown. Last, but not the least." He was the largest one of them in both height and weight, brown hair, mustache, and brown eyes.

As each man said his name, he stepped forward another step. Sullivan and Boyd moved toward them and shook each hand.

"We're glad to met y'all. Me and Boyd here come here from Austin. He's spent all his time out of there. I started there and also up in Dallas a few years, then back to Austin most recent. We been down to Brownsville on an assignment, and then was sent over here. We was sorry to hear about yore captain and sergeant. It is a dangerous thing we do as you well know. We both lost a lot friends, more than I care to recall.

"We won't be like yore other leaders were, I don't guess. But you'll get used to us. Quickly, I hope. We won't never ask you to do somethin' we ain't willing to do. You got any problem, you come to us. Don't hold it back. There ain't nothin' you gonna face or have to deal with that we ain't already seen.

"We have fought and killed Comanches, Comancheros, bank robbers, killers, and Apache, but not so many of them. Ran into some of them way down south recently. You Boys might have to educate us on them.

"Now, does anybody have any questions or anything you want to say?

There was a pause. Everybody looked around. No one said anything.

"All right. Me and Boyd need to go out to the fort in the morning and see the commander there. Tim Davis, how about you go with us, see us out there since you been there before?"

"Yes, Sir, Captain. Be glad to."

"Thanks. And one thing more. From now on, no more Yes, Sir, and no more Captain. You can call me Toombs or Sullivan. Same is true for Boyd. We're in this together. We will eat, sleep, travel, fight together. We might even die together. So let's keep it informal. When I die, I want a friend holding my hand, not a subject.

"All right, me and Boyd got to settle in. See ya around tomorrow."

"Uh, Captain, uh, I mean, Sullivan," said Billy Crowe, "if ya get what ya want off your horses and the mule, I'll take them down to the livery for ya."

"Oh, good. Thanks so much."

Then the three of them turned and went out to the
street.

Chapter Seven

The next morning, Sullivan, Boyd, and Davis rode out to Fort Bliss.

As they came to the gate of the fort, Timony Davis nodded at the guard standing there and lifted his hand in a half wave. The guard waved them on in, recognizing Davis.

They stopped in front of the office building, tied their horses at the rail, and approached the front door. Davis spoke to the guard standing there.

"Texas Rangers here to see the colonel."

The guard opened the door, saying, "Go on in."

When they entered, a young officer sitting at a table stood up.

"I'm Corporal Davis, Texas Rangers. This is Captain Toombs Sullivan and Sergeant William Boyd. Here to see the colonel."

"Just a moment, please."

The young man knocked on the door, opened it, and spoke.

"Texas Rangers here to see you, Sir."

"Show them in."

"Right this way."

The three Rangers entered the office. The man behind the big desk stood up.

"Davis, good to see you again."

"Thank you, Sir. This is Captain Toombs Sullivan and Sergeant William Boyd."

The colonel came around his desk to speak to them and shake their hands.

"I'm Anthony Kicklighter. Pleased to meet you. Have a seat. Have a seat."

Colonel Anthony Kicklighter was an impressive looking man. He was six feet tall, trim, in good physical condition it appeared. He had dark hair, slicked back, and handle-bar sideburns. He was a polished graduate of West Point Military Academy, and had been a young General in the Civil War. He had been born and raised in Pennsylvania.

When the four of them were seated, the colonel handed over to them a box of cigars. They each took one and so did Kicklighter. He lit his, and handed them a little china jar holding matches.

When all of the cigars were lit, a cloud of smoke rose slowly toward the ceiling.

"Welcome to west Texas."

"Thank you, Sir," Sullivan replied.

"I got word you were coming here. I was sorry about your predecessors. This is a hard country we are in. I suppose you would like for me to tell you all the latest about this area."

"That would be helpful," Sullivan said.

"Where to begin? El Paso was nothing but a gateway, a small gateway, into Mexico, a pass. Mostly Mexicans lived here. A few whites. This fort has been here about twenty years. After the war, people began their push west. The land of opportunity. A good opportunity to get yourself robbed, killed, kidnapped. But regardless of that, the population just kept on increasing.

"So the government, meaning the Army, started pushing the

Indians out, over into Mexico and trying to put them on reservations. The Indians did not like that very much. They started fighting back, and they still are.

"Your reputation, Captain Sullivan, goes before you. I know you have been fighting Indians down through these volatile years. So I'm not telling you something you don't already know."

"Well, Sir, I have been at it a while. I have never been here, but I have been all down the lower part of west Texas. Yes, I have seen it all, and quite frankly, I have done it all too. Done too much of it, I'm afraid. I killed so many I could not begin to count them up. Boyd here's been at it as well. We both know what we have gotten into. And, well, that's what they pay us to do. So we do it."

"Now Sullivan, you will find that El Paso can be a wild town for the reasons we are talking about. All these new people. The town Marshal is Ted Wheeler. He has two deputies, Sam Fears and Jackson Barns. But the three of them sometime get swamped, as they say. They will call on you for help. I know your job is protecting whites from Indians, but you will sometime be protecting whites from whites and sometime Mexicans from whites and vice versa. So just be aware of that."

"Yes, I have done that before too. Sometime whites are worse than Indians. We'll take it as it comes."

"Good. What else?"

"Any trouble spots right now?"

"Not today. Not as of this hour, but that could change any moment."

"How well we know."

"Ranger Boyd, do you have anything?"

"No, Sir. I think I see where we are and what it is. I'm fine for now. And yes, that could change any moment as well."

Colonel Kicklighter laughed the laughter of a confident man who also knows how doubtful things can suddenly become.

"How about a sip of brandy?" he asked.

"Why not?" Sullivan replied.

Chapter Eight

As the three Rangers were about to mount their horses, Sullivan said, "Why don't we go have a talk with Marshall Wheeler, and find out what he has to say?"

"Sounds like a good idea to me," replied Boyd.

They rode back into town and found the streets were bustling with wagons, horses, shoppers, cowboys, and women with their children.

"A busy place," Boyd observed.

"Pretty much all day right up till about mid-night," Tim Davis responded.

"Better than bein' a dead town. They ain't no fun at all," Sullivan said.

"Not a'tall," Boyd agreed.

When they reached the Marshal's office and jail, they dismounted and tied their horses.

They walked inside, and saw a man sitting at a desk looking through some papers.

"You Marshal Wheeler?" Sullivan asked.

"I am so far today," he replied.

"I'm Toombs Sullivan, and this is William Boyd. You know Davis here."

"Sullivan, Boyd. I been expecting you fellers. Glad to see you, more than you know and could imagine."

"Sounds like trouble," Boyd said.

"Ha ha," Wheeler laughed. "Trouble is my first name, middle name, and last name. And my mailing address is El Trouble. I only quit on Mondays. What is today? Oh, well, not today. Have a seat, Boys."

Marshall Ted Wheeler stood up. He appeared to be near fifty years old, if not older. He was stout looking, partial gray hair, clean-shaven. He wore black pants, a white shirt, a black string-tie. He was wearing a belt high holding his holster and pistol.

The four of them sat down. Sullivan looked closely at Wheeler.

"What is yore trouble today?" Sullivan asked.

"You see this stack of papers? They ain't no invitations to no dinner parties. I got twenty-seven wanted posters right here. And these are just the latest."

"Any Indian trouble right now?"

"Not that I know of."

"It's my understanding that when there's no Indian trouble, we sometime help you out. When you need it bad."

"I need it bad right now. There's three of us. And we can't all three work twenty-four hours a day. That means two of us at either day or night and one of us at either day or night."

"What's the worst trouble you got right now?"

Marshall Wheeler fumbled through his wanted posters and pulled out one.

"See this man? That's Jack the Beast Stalker. Don't think that is his real last name. It's something like Armstrong, Armistead, or something. He got the name Stalker because he is a hired gun who likes to stalk his victims. He kills for a purpose and a price. He also robs banks, stagecoaches, stores, settlers, what and whoever is at hand and available.

"Where is he most of the time?" Sullivan asked.

"We don't rightly know. That's a big part of the problem. He's like an Indian. He strikes out of nowhere, hit and run, and then hides out. We just can't go get him."

"Who does he have with him?"

"Oh, he has a gang, a gang of killers. Made up of a mixture. Couple of whites. Couple of Mexicans. Couple of Indians. We don't know how many. Some witnesses say seven or eight. Some say ten, twenty. Others say fifty, an army. I doubt that many. I would guess between eight and fifteen, twenty at most, just from what I have seen and heard."

"What does he look like?"

"He's Jack the Beast. He's a beast all right. Big, tall, big shoulders. Dark complexion. May be a mixture of races, don't know. Has a dark full beard. Long dark hair, shoulder length. Dark eyes. Wears a big black hat, dark clothing. A black coat. Buffalo fur coat in the winter. Carries two pistols. Yellowboy rifle. Good with knives. Likes to use them. Rides a big black horse.

"His men are as well armed as he is, I understand.

"He steals cattle. Trades with the Indians. They trade with Comancheros. They sell them to the Army. Sometime the Army buys back from them their own cattle."

"Oh, I have seen that before. I've never understood why the Army does that. They keep the cycle going."

"It's supply and demand. The Army needs them to feed their men. They can supply. No mystery there."

"Yeah, that's true."

"That's about all I know."

"All right. Me and Boyd just got here, so we need a day or two to kind'a settle in. But we'll be on alert. Any news or report about the Beast, let us know. We'll go after him."

"Good. I'm glad you're here."

"Fine," Sullivan replied. He wasn't sure he was glad to be there, and he was not going to say he was.

Chapter Nine

Four days later, Marshal Wheeler came busting into the hotel just as Sullivan and Boyd were finishing breakfast in the dining room.

"Where's Captain Sullivan?" he exclaimed in a loud voice.

The desk clerk made no reply, simply pointing toward the dining room.

Sullivan and Boyd heard him and waved.

Wheeler approached them quickly.

"We got trouble!" he almost yelled.

"What happened?" Sullivan asked, as he stood up, finishing his cup of coffee.

"Two ranchers down the river have been hit. Hit hard. Burned out. That's all I was told. Don't know what happened to them."

"We'll get after that right now. Exactly where?"

"There's an old mission down there, about twenty-five, thirty mile. Those places are on beyond there, not far."

"Get the men, Boyd."

Boyd wiped his mouth with his napkin, got up, and rushed out of the room.

"It'll take us an hour at least to get ourselves together, but we'll be on our way as soon as we can."

"Welcome to west Texas."

"Thanks. I think."

Nearly two hours later, ten Rangers on ten horses trailing two pack-mules rode out of El Paso headed south along the river.

Sullivan was thinking, well, here I am, at it again. But I don't have to be here. I didn't have to do this. However, I was born for this, I think, equipped for this. I can do this. I think I was born for this. Hope I ain't wrong.

They had ridden hard, and about noon, or a little later, they came by the old Spanish mission. It had been there for a long time, it was obvious. But it was still in operation. They saw several people milling around.

The river was off to their right a few hundred yards.

Sullivan halted the men soon after passing the mission.

"Davis!" he called out, "Take the point, and see if you can find one of those ranches."

"I'm on it," Davis said, as he rode on past Sullivan and Boyd, galloping away.

Thirty minutes later, they began seeing smoke rising in the distance and Davis coming back toward them. He stopped and waved them on.

"Let's go, Boys!" Sullivan shouted.

They charged ahead and soon reached Davis.

"Found it. A bad scene."

"It figgers. Take us in."

As they headed toward the ranch, Sullivan rehearsed it all. He rolled it over and over in his mind. He had seen it all before, many times. He knew exactly what they would find. He dreaded it, and wanted to turn around and go back to El Paso. But no, this was the job. It was his job. He had to go on ahead.

Soon they were there. The smoke they had seen came from the large barn, still smoldering from the fire the day before. The house was still warm, but mostly the fire was out. Only a couple of little streams of smoke rose up skyward.

They dismounted and all the Rangers stood there looking at what was before them. There were three bodies on the ground. They had been shot in the head, throats cut, hands tied behind their backs.

Finally, after a few minutes Sullivan asked a question.

"What do you not see?"

Boyd knew what it was, and what Sullivan was seeking. But he held back, waiting to see who would speak up and what he would say.

"Three males," Davis answered, "a man and two boys, and no women."

"That's right," Sullivan said. "No women. There must have been women here, females, grown or otherwise, and they are gone now. Look around, Boys, see what you find, what we can learn about this mess. Then we'll put these fellers in the ground."

Sullivan looked over at Boyd, and motioned for him to follow.

"Let's me and you look for footprints and tracks."

They walked toward what was left of the front of the house, a pile of burned timbers and stones.

"It's pretty clear right here," Boyd said, as he pointed to the ground. "Look at all this. Boots. No moccasins. Course, some Indians, Comanches, wear boots now, sometime Army issue off some dead cavalrymen."

"Yeah. My guess, these ain't them. These are boots worn by whites. Let's look for their horses. Look over there. Shod horses. No Indian ponies at all."

"You thinking what I'm thinking?" Boyd asked.

"Yep. Jack the Beast Stalker. Look over there."

They walked around to the far side of the house. There on the ground they found part of a dress, torn almost into.

"At least one female," Boyd said.

Sullivan picked it up.

"Let's go see what the others have found."

They walked back around toward the barn.

"What'cha got, Boys?" Sullivan asked.

When the group came back together, Davis spoke for them.

"We found quite a bit of boot traffic. Must have been whites or Mexicans. And a lot of horse tracks coming out of the corral. There must have been twenty or more horses in there. They all head off south of here, looks like."

"And that's where we're headed, right after them," Sullivan replied. "What else ya got?"

"Found some female's clothing, two different colors. Must have been two of them."

"That makes three. Found this over there. And no Indian pony tracks anywhere that we see. All right, Boys, let's get'em in the ground. Least we can give'em a decent burial and send them home."

The men took a few shovels off the mules. They dug three graves beyond the burned down barn. They placed the bodies in the graves and covered them over. A couple of the men fashioned three crosses for the graves. Then they all gathered around.

Sullivan looked over at Boyd and nodded his head. Boyd read the Twenty-third Psalm. Then Sullivan prayed.

"God, they belong to you anyway. We givin'em back to ya. Take'em in and give them a nice welcome. Amen."

Chapter Ten

When the Rangers left that first ranch, they followed the tracks on south. It was easy to see the tracks made by their horses and the ones they stole.

Sullivan sent Slim Pardue to ride point. It was not long until he returned.

"I found the other place. Bout four miles ahead I reckon. Nothing left there. I did not go in real close, but I didn't see no people lying around."

"Good," Sullivan replied. "Maybe they got away. Take us on in."

As they headed south, Pardue led them on. They all knew they would soon come to the other ranch that had been raided. Though no one said anything, they secretly dreaded what they might find.

It did not take long. They saw no smoke this time, but there was a house and a barn and also an out-building that had been burned down. They dismounted and began looking around.

"Must have hit this one first, since there was no smoke," Boyd said. "Burned out quicker."

"Yep, and that means they came here from the south. So maybe they have a place where they live down that way. They were headed right back down there when they left the other place.

"Look around, Boys!"

They all began looking at the ground for tracks and for anything else they could find.

A couple of the men went to the other side of what was left of the barn.

"Over here!" they called out.

Sullivan, Boyd, and the others went to where the two men were standing. Before they got there, they could see what they had found.

There were five bodies lying together, side by side. There was a man, a woman, and three young boys, all shot in the head.

"How could somebody do such a thing?" Tim Davis asked.

"It's easy for killers," answered Tommy Crowe. "If ya got what they want, they just kill ya and take it."

"That's about the size of it, Tommy," said Sullivan.

"On over away from the house on the other side, I found where they had camped for the night," Tommy Crown said. "I guess that's why we saw no smoke from here because they hit it the day before the other one. There's ashes from a couple of fires where they cooked. Looks like they had a cow maybe or something they had butchered at some point. Maybe they took some beef from that out-building.”

“That explains it. All right, get the shovels. You know what we gotta do.”

Five graves were dug. The bodies were placed in them. When they were covered over, Sullivan handed the Bible to Tim Davis.

“The Twenty-third.”

After he finished reading the Psalm, Sullivan turned toward Boyd.

“You pray this time.”

“Sure. Our Heavenly Father, receive unto Thyself these thine own faithful servants, granting them their everlasting home with you and all the Saints and all who have gone before us. In the Holy names of the Father, the Son, and the Holy Spirit. Amen.”

“Thanks to you Tim, Boyd. Glad we had this moment of prayer over these innocent folks. Glad we felt a little religious there for a bit.

“Time now to feel something else. And that something else is hatred. Hatred for what these men did to two families. Hatred for their kind. And with a perfect hatred we are gonna find them and kill them. There won’t be no talk of bringing them to justice and giving them a fair trial.

"We are justice, and we will administer judgement and punishment. Do not hold back. Kill them. You catch one of them unarmed, shoot him where he stands, sits, or lies.

"Don't anybody come to me and say, I got one over here tied up, unless by tied up you mean he is hanging from a tree.

"Questions anybody?"

Sullivan paused for a moment to see if anyone had a question or comment.

"All right, you know what to do. Let's go do it. Mount up. Cap Bridges take the point."

The Rangers got on their horses, with Bridges riding off quickly ahead of them.

They continued to follow the tracks as they rode along not far from the river.

They kept following the tracks all day. They could not tell if that group of raiders had ever slowed down or stopped to rest. It looked like they had not.

Late in the evening, Cap Bridges came back to report.

"They just keep going on and on."

"Yep," Sullivan replied. "We need to stop and make camp though. Boys! Let's move over to the river for the night."

Chapter Eleven

The horses and the mules were allowed to drink from the river. They had not had any water all day.

Then the packs and two folding tables were taken off the mules as they and the horses were tied to trees. Two fires were started, the tables set up, and the meal was prepared.

After they were through eating, most of the men walked to the edge of the river, took off their boots and clothes, and waded out into the water. It was a refreshing change after the long hot and dusty day.

Boyd set up a schedule for guards, one on each end of their camp.

As the sun went down, the Rangers sat around the fires cleaning the dust off of their weapons and saddles.

Boyd was seated next to Sullivan. He spoke in a low voice.

"Did you get the feeling we were being watched all day, or most of it, and maybe being followed?"

"Yeah, I did. But that happens so much. There's always somebody who picks up the dust we stir up. Mostly Indians, I think, because they always want our horses. You can bet one of them will come in here tonight and see what he can get away

with. Better alert the Boys."

Boyd got up and began moving around the camp talking to the men. Then he went to the two of them that were on guard duty.

When he reached Tommy Crown on the upper end, he stopped and looked around and especially across the river.

"Heard anything, Tommy?"

"Nope. Quiet as can be."

"Be aware we may have visitors. Me and Sullivan think we was being observed all day."

"Indians?"

"Yep. Maybe."

"Want horses?"
"Yep. Maybe."

"Shoot on sight?"

"Yep. Definitely."

Boyd went to the other end of the camp to speak to Billy Crowe. It was much the same conversation.

Then he came back to where Sullivan was standing near the fire.

"I just got a bad feeling. Worse than today. Maybe I'm just jumpy. I keep looking across the river and also off toward the east. There's just somebody out there."

"Why don't me and you go find out. Get yore rifle. Don't act like you're going somewhere. Just be cleaning yore rifle, looking at it. Walk toward the river. Then circle around in the dark and meet me over there to the east a ways. I'll do the same and go down the other way and around. Don't shoot me. Warn Tommy where we are. I'll warn Billy."

Sullivan and Boyd slowly wandered around toward the river, and then disappeared in the shadows.

Five minute later, they met in the dark.

"Let's move real slow and careful," Sullivan whispered.

They edged their way forward, listening for any kind of sound. They stopped, listened, moved slowly forward. Nothing. They heard nothing.

They stood still for ten minutes. There was not a sound, not a night-bird, not a rustling by small animals, not a breeze blowing leaves on the trees.

Sullivan shrugged his shoulders and shook his head. Boyd shook his head. Then Sullivan whispered.

"I think there's nobody here. Maybe we are just jumpy."

"Yeah. Jumpy."

"Let's swing around by Tommy. See if he heard anything at all."

They still moved quietly through the small trees and brush.

"It's us, Tommy," Sullivan called out.

There was no reply. Sullivan and Boyd looked at each other.

"Tommy."

Still there was nothing, no reply. They moved on toward the river.

Then there was Tommy! Lying on the ground!

"Run check on Billy!" Sullivan said.

As Boyd rushed along the river and through the camp, Sullivan rolled Tommy Crown over. His throat had been cut. Blood was all over him.

Sullivan left him and ran toward the camp.

"What is it?" Tim Davis asked excitedly.

"Tommy's dead!"

"What?"

Sullivan reached Boyd and found him looking down. Billy Crowe was lying on the ground. His throat was cut.

Sullivan and Boyd looked at each other. Sorrow, fear, sadness, anger was all over their faces.

"Let's go tell the Boys," Sullivan said.

By the time they reached the camp, all the men were standing up, their pistols in their hands.

"Bad news, Boys," Sullivan said, as he and Boyd reached them. "Somebody killed Tommy and Billy, cut their throats. Davis, go count the horses. Y'all go get those Boys and bring them here by the fire. We'll bury them in the mornin'. Be careful. Watch out."

Soon Davis came back from where the horses were.

"Two horses missing. Who ya think did it? Comanche, Apache, those raiders?"

Sullivan thought a moment, and then spit in the fire.

"I'm guessing Comanche. They love horses, and will kill anybody to get them."

Minutes later, the two men were laid by the fire. The Rangers stood around looking at them

"A proper send-off in the mornin', Boys," Sullivan said. "Get some sleep if you can. Any volunteers for taking the next watch? No. I'll do it."

"Me too," Boyd added.

Chapter Twelve

The next day, two graves were dug by the river. Tommy Crown and Billy Crowe were gently placed in them. The dirt was slowly raked over them. Two crosses were put in place.

Sullivan stood before the graves and before the Rangers.

"These two young men lost their lives for Texas and for us.

They didn't give their lives for Texas. I don't want to hear anybody sayin' that. Their lives were taken from them without permission, without askin' them, without mercy, brutally taken

from them.

"This changes everything for the rest of us. Our mission was to go after the raiders. That has changed now. We will not let this pass. We are going after whoever took the lives of our friends here.

"They were fine young men, taken away in the very flower of their youth. We won't stand for that. We will not accept that. We will get their killers, and will get our revenge.

"Vengeance is mine saith the Lord. Vengeance will be ours. Davis, read the Bible now. Then Boyd, you pray."

Timothy Davis read the Twenty-third Psalm. William Boyd prayed.

"Oh, God, receive these thy young servants into thy kingdom. Give them eternal rest and blessings. Christ name. Amen."

"Break camp, Boys, except for you, Davis and Boyd. Go find which way they went. We'll be along."

When everything was loaded on the mules and the horses were made ready, the Rangers mounted up.

"Let's move along," Sullivan said.

They headed out after Boyd and Davis, following the tracks they made. After they had traveled for a bout a mile, they found Boyd and Davis waiting on them.

"A lot of tracks right here," Boyd said.

"I see," Sullivan observed, as he looked at the ground.

"Our two are mixed with a lot of Indian ponies. Looks like a larger band was staying here waiting on them to come back with the horses. They go on off to the south."

"All right," Sullivan replied. "Go on after them. We'll be along."

They followed the tracks all morning. About noon, Boyd and Davis came to a place where the tracks turned toward the river.

When Sullivan and the others arrived there, they found them watering their horses. They dismounted and did the same.

"They went across into Mexico," Boyd said.

"Well, that does it, I guess. We can't be going into Mexico, can we Boyd?"

"Nope. If we was to do that, it would cause an international stink, and we would lose our jobs with the Rangers."

"We can't have that. They'll come back over here, and we will get them for sure."

"We did cross the trail of the raiders back there."

"Yeah, we saw that. Well, let's get back after them. They got those women we need to try to save. Lead out, Davis."

They returned to their pursuit of the raiders led by Jack the Beast Stalker.

Three hours later, Davis came riding back toward them. He stopped and shook his head.

"I found'em. It ain't a purdy sight."

"Show us," Sullivan said.

They followed Davis for almost a mile. They came to a place with tall trees. It looked like they had camped there for the night. There were places where there had been five campfires. And it was obvious many horses had been held there.

And the women.

They found the women.

The nude bodies of both of them were hanging from the limb of a tree. They had been raped, beaten, and shot in the head.

The Rangers sat on their horses looking at them. No one said anything. They were struck by the brutality they saw.

Finaly, after what seemed like many minutes, but probably were not, Davis spoke.

"How? Why?"

"Don't try to understand killers," Sullivan said. "You'll bust a blood vessel in yore brain. It's what they do. And if this country is ever going to be civilized, then we have to kill all the killers. You can't make peace with'em and get along and be nice. Just kill'em."

There was more silence as the men thought about what they saw and what Sullivan said. They knew he was right. Just kill them all.

"Well, you know what to do. Get'em down and in the ground."

The Rangers dug two graves in the shade of the trees. They wrapped the women in what was left of their clothing. They gently placed them in the graves. They covered them over. They looked at Sullivan.

"Davis and Boyd, read and pray."

As they began, Sullivan walked away from them toward the river. He stopped fifty yards away. He could hear them. When they were finished, he came back to the group.

"We'll make camp over there by the river. Can't be no sleepin' in this place."

The men put their hats back on and walked away.

Chapter Thirteen

The next day, the tracking of the raiders continued. Now the Rangers were even more determined to catch up with them. None more than Sullivan.

"Boyd, I want you to ride point this time. I got a funny feelin'. I don't know. Maybe I'm just jumpy."

"Maybe not."

"I just need you out there."

"Sure."

"Be careful."

"You bet."

As Boyd rode off, Sullivan wondered if he had done the right thing. He felt he needed Boyd's experience out ahead, yet he was also concerned something might happen to him.

"Boys, let's get on after them," Sullivan said.

The Rangers mounted their horses and followed Boyd and the tracks he followed.

Sullivan kept thinking about what might be ahead. He had done this too many times. If the raiders knew they were coming, then they would probably set up an ambush. Sullivan had been ambushed many times before, but he always found a way to defeat his enemies whoever they were. The trick was to ambush the ambushers. That meant outsmarting them, going around behind them or coming at them from both sides behind their back. Boyd knew all about that. He would size it up for them and come back with a plan, an idea, a suggestion for Sullivan to mull over.

The hours dragged by as the Rangers ate dust and sweated from the heat and wiped both from their faces with their sleaves. Sullivan stopped them.

"Get off and rest a bit, you and the horses."

Sullivan walked around on the hot dirt and looked at all the tracks. It was impossible to tell how many they were following. Boyd would know.

Late in the evening Boyd came back to them.

"I caught up with'em," Boyd said, as he dismounted. "They in a grove of live oak trees about two mile ahead. Beddin' down for the night."

"How many ya think?" Sullivan asked.

"Hard to tell. Didn't want to get too close. But I'd say twenty to thirty at least."

"More than I was countin' on,"

"How ya want to play it?"

"I need to think a minute. Where their horses?"

"Off to the east of the grove there's a little stream, which is why they stopped there, I'm guessin'. They got their horses tied out near there."

"Makes sense. Probably been there before. All right, Boys, dismount. Stretch it out some."

Sullivan and Boyd walked away from the men a little way.

"Boyd, let's split the group, first of all. What ya think, sundown, midnight, or dawn?"

"I like the dawn when they are still asleep or half asleep."

"I think you're right. I'll come in from the east with the sun in their eyes. When they react to us, then you hit'em from the west with their backs to ya."

"Good idea."

"Let's tell the Boys."

They walked back to where the men were standing with the horses and the mules.

"Gather around. They're up ahead, camped for the night in a grove of trees. We gonna hit'em at dawn. Easom, Canton, Pardue, Bridges will be with me. We'll come at them from the east with the sun to our backs and in their face. Davis, Hanson, English, Dickens will be with Boyd from the west at their backs after the shootin' starts. Now, be careful about shootin' each other. Don't shoot wild. Pick ya target.

"This ain't a very good place to bed down. We'll go over to the river to water and eat and rest some. Then some time after midnight we'll come back right here and wait."

It was not far to the river. When they got there, they watered the horses, took the saddles off to let them rest, and then tied them off. They prepared a meal, but ate it cold, not wanting to start a fire, create smoke, and attract attention.

They laid down to rest and perhaps sleep a little. The hours dragged by, like always when you are waiting for something you have to do.

Sullivan did not lie down. He sat by the fire, walked down to the river, checked on the horses, counted the minutes as they crawled on by.

At twelve-thirty, he alerted the men that it was time to go back where they were. They would wait there. As soon as there was any hint of gray breaking into the black of darkness, they would get in position for their raid on the raiders.

They saddled their horses, mounted up, and moved out slowly and quietly. They left the mules where they were tied to small trees.

When they arrived at the trail, Sullivan signaled his men to follow him. Boyd did the same, as both groups got themselves closer to where they needed to be. There they dismounted again and waited.

Chapter Fourteen

Sullivan kept looking back toward the east, nervously waiting the first hint of daybreak. Finally, he saw it, the faintest little streak of light in the eastern sky. He whispered to the men.

"Mount up. We'll move over closer, more in line. Stay outside that grove of trees until we get there. We'll see just where they are, and then let'em have it. Watch for Boyd and his men. Don't shoot them. Let's go."

When they were on their horses, they slowly walked them to the south three hundred yards. They stopped when they got where they could faintly see the trees. They sat there waiting.

The sky began to lighten up now. They could see the trees clearly.

Suddenly there was warmth on their backs. Brighter and brighter the new day became.

Sullivan pulled out his pistol and held it up in the air. The other Rangers pulled their pistols. They were all ready to attack.

Pow!

Pow!

Pow!

Bang!

Bang!

Pow!

The gun-fire was coming from where Boyd was!

It was too soon!

Too quick!

Pow!

Pow!

Pow!

Gunfire from behind Sullivan!

Two of Sullivan's men fell from their horses!

"Turn around!" Sullivan shouted.

Pow!

Pow!

Pow!

Sullivan and his men began firing back!

"Let's get out of here!" he yelled.

They spurred their horses and retreated back toward where they had been!

The raiders followed them shooting wildly with pistols and rifles!

Pow!

Bang!

Pow!

Pow!

Bang!

"Dismount! Take cover!"

Sullivan and the men with him had pulled out their rifles and began firing them accurately! Raiders fell to the ground!

Suddenly they heard gunshots from their right!

Pow!

Pow!

Pow!

It was Boyd and his men coming to help them!

The raiders drew back and disappeared.

Boyd and Davis rode up to where Sullivan and his men were.

"Thanks," Sullivan said. "Where are the others?"

"They're dead. Jumped us before we knew what hit us."

"We lost two."

"They all left, headed across the river to Mexico."

Sullivan stood there silently for a moment, looking down at the ground.

"It's my fault. Bad planning, I guess. My fault."

"Nope," Boyd replied. "Ain't no fault except them raiders. They the ones that killed our men. Their fault."

"Thanks for tryin', but it don't do no good."

"What now?"

"Let's get our Boys in the ground. We'll bury them near those live oaks. Somebody go get the mules so we'll have the shovels."

"I'll go," Davis said.

"Good. Let's gather them up."

The Rangers went to retrieve the bodies of their fallen comrades. They carried them to the grove of trees. By the time they had them there, Davis returned with the mules.

Five graves were dug. Into those graves were placed the bodies of Hanson, Pardue, English, Bridges, and Dickens. When the dirt was over them, the Rangers stood looking at the graves.

No one said anything. They were waiting on Sullivan to say something, but he was silent.

Finally, Boyd read the Psalm and said the prayer.

"God, these men died bravely in the line of duty for this state and this country to make this a better place for people to live. Receive them. They are yours. Amen."

Sullivan looked up, waited a moment, and spoke.

"I'm sorry, Boys. It's my fault. I bout destroyed this company. You expect better of me and should have it. I just might resign."

Sullivan turned to walk to his horse.

"What about these dead raiders? We gonna bury them?" Davis asked.

Sullivan made no response. He kept walking.

"Nope," said Boyd. "We'll let'em rot. The animals can eat'em. We always leave the dead lie. Come on, Boys. We're goin' home now."

Chapter Fifteen

After the other men had left the breakfast table in the hotel dining room, Sullivan slowly sipped his third cup of coffee.

"Well, William, we got to find us some more men now. Guess we could get some notices printed up and put'em around town, and also put a thing in the El Paso Herald."

"Maybe that will get us some attention."

"We'll see."

Later that day, Sullivan went to the newspaper office where he met the owner and publisher, Archibald Covington. He had fifty handbills printed and the same notice put in the paper.

TEXAS RANGERS NOW HIRING

Young Men Wanted, Must Be Single

Good With Guns, Have Own Horse

Good Pay

See Toombs Sullivan, El Paso Hotel

Sullivan and Boyd placed the handbills all over town. Then they waited for men to come and apply for the job.

They sat out front of the hotel on a bench every afternoon. They sat at the dinning room table and drank coffee all morning. They sat in the hotel parlor and read the newspaper, looking over and over at the ad.

"Maybe I worded it wrong," Sullivan said.

"Nope."

"Maybe it don't say enough."

"Nope."

"Maybe it says too much."

"Nope."

"Maybe nobody wants to be a Texas Ranger."

"Yep."

"Maybe they heard about half of us gettin' killed."

"Yep."

"Maybe my name on the ad scares them all away."

"Nope."

"Maybe I should'a put yore name on it."

"Nope."

Two weeks of that went by with no takers, no curiosity, no questions, no inquiries, no applicants, nothing.

"What do ya think is the problem?" Sullivan asked one afternoon, as he and Boyd sat on the bench outside, trying to stay awake.

"Nobody wants to be a Texas Ranger here in El Paso. It's the culture."

"The culture?" Sullivan asked.

"Yeah, it's the culture, you know, the way people here live. We see young men around town, and ya would think some of them would make fine Rangers, but they don't want to be lawmen. They want to drink, play poker, chase women and catch some of'em. They want to find a way to get rich, discover gold, rob a bank, marry a woman with money. Rangerin' ain't for none of these fellers here in El Paso."

"Got any bright ideas, Boyd?"

"Nope. Got no ideas, bright, dull, or otherwise."

Meanwhile the three other Rangers who were left, Timothy Davis, Charles Easom, and Eddie Canton spent their time cleaning, polishing, and shining their pistols, rifles, knives, boots, saddles, bridles, and everything else they could think of. When they got tired of cleaning their own, they cleaned, polished, and shined those of Sullivan and Boyd. Nothing any of them ever had ever looked so good.

Every few days, a report came in about a farm or ranch being raided either by the raiders led by Jack the Beast Stalker or Apaches or Comanches or Comancheros.

Sullivan felt guilty about not responding to these reports, but he did not want the five of them to try to take on an unknown number of Indians or whites or Comancheros made up of both.

"I got an idea," Sullivan said one afternoon, as he and Boyd sat on the bench outside in front of the hotel. "I think I'll go to Austin, and see what I can get done there. Maybe I can recruit some men there or maybe Pendergrass will transfer some men to us. Nobody needs good men more than what we do."

"It's a mighty long way," Boyd replied. His feet were propped up, his hat down over his face, his hands clasped together across his chest.

"Yep. It is that. A long way."

"Very long."

"Yep."

Nothing was said for a few minutes. Sullivan looked up and down the street. He spit at a fly he saw on the boardwalk near his feet. He missed.

"Think I'll go anyway."

"Figured."

"Leave in a couple of days."

"Good timing."

"Timing is everything."

"Yep."

Chapter Sixteen

Three days later, Sullivan headed out for El Paso. He waited an extra day so he could travel east with Buck McFalls and his freight wagons. It would be best for both if they were together, but McFalls would probably not have any trouble. His wagons were loaded down with cotton headed for the coast. No raiders or Indians or robbers or thieves would want that.

After nearly a week on the road, they arrived in Austin. Sullivan went straight to Ranger headquarters to see Major

Pendergrass.

"Come in Sullivan. Have a seat. Got your report in your letter. Sorry about the misfortune you all experienced. It's a tough business in a hard country."

"That it is. How are you?"

"We're doing fine here. The usual problems that go with this work. You know."

"I do know."

"Yeah."

"We need some replacements. Five at least. We've not been able to recruit anybody over there. So that's why I'm here."

"Figured. Wish I could give you some men from some other companies, but we are hard pressed all way around. We'll have to do what you did there. I'll get something in the paper and some posters around town. We'll see what happens. You get some rest."

"Yeah. Thanks. I'll check in tomorrow."

"Fine."

Sullivan left the office and headed straight for the hotel he usually stayed in. The man at the desk knew him. Sullivan approached him when he went through the door.

"Need a room. Back in town a few days."

"Sure, Mister Sullivan," the man said, as he turned around to get the key. "Say, there's a letter here for you from some lady who left it. I told her you were in and out, but

I didn't know when you'd be back."

He handed the envelope to Sullivan.

"Oh, thanks," he replied, as he took the key in his left hand and the letter in his right.

As Sullivan turned to walk away, he looked down at the letter. His name was on the front of the envelope. The handwriting was unmistakable.

He quickly tore the envelope open, unfolded the letter, and saw the words.

My Darling Toombs,

I am here in Austin teaching school. I came here

knowing that at some point you would be here

because

Ranger headquarters is here. I have a room at Mrs.

Alice Higginbottom's rooming house. Anyone at the

hotel

can tell you where the school is and where the

boarding

house is.

All my love,

Constance

Sullivan's hands were shaking as he read the letter
again.

He had found her, and was astonished because he
found her without looking for her. Maybe she found him.
He caught his breath, swallowed hard, and turned around.

"Where's the school?"

"You go out, turn left, go down near the end of the
street, turn left again. You'll see the school over there
near the church, just past."

"Thanks."

He had not yet put his horse in the stable, so he rushed out, got on the horse, and raced down the street, taking a left toward the school.

When he reached the school, he jumped off the horse, tied him at the rail, and went to the door. He looked inside. There were two large rooms. On the right side he saw a teacher and a room full of older students, perhaps twelve to sixteen he thought. He looked in the room on the left, and there he saw a large group of younger students, and there was Constance standing in front of them, her back to a blackboard. There were large numbers written all over the board.

When she saw Sullivan, her mouth dropped open. Then she spoke to the children.

"Write your numbers, Children. I'll be right back. Now all quiet, please."

She walked up the aisle toward him. When she reached him, he grabbed her, pulled her outside to the stoop, put his arms around her, and kissed her madly.

"What time you get through here?"

"Three o'clock."

"I'll meet you at your place."

"No, not there," she answered. "Mrs. Higginbottom is very strict about men coming to her house."

"Come to the hotel. Room two eleven. I'll be waiting on you."

"I'll be there soon as I can."

"Good."

Sullivan watched her as she went back to her room.

Then he got on his horse, and went to the livery stable.

He put his horse in a stall, threw his saddle on the wall of the stall, pulled his rifles and saddle bags off, and told the man there he would pay him when he left. The owner knew Sullivan, so that was fine.

Sullivan walked to the hotel and room two eleven.

Chapter Seventeen

Sullivan rolled over and looked at the clock. It was nearly five p.m., so he got up and began dressing.

"I'll go down and get us a table in the dining room, and give you some time to dress and pretty up."

"All right. I'll be down there soon."

Sullivan left Constance in his room and went downstairs. He walked in the dining room and found a table off in a far corner.

He sat down. The waitress came over to take his order.

"Oh, there'll be two of us, but how about two coffees, and we'll order when she gets here."

"Fine. I'll be right back."

In a few minutes, Constance came down the stairs, entered the dining room, and spotted Sullivan. He stood up and waved.

When she reached him, he pulled out her chair and helped her be seated.

"Guess we got a lot to talk about," he said.

"I guess so."

"We both been through a lot."

"Yes, we have," she agreed.

"I'm sorry you lost your husband, and I'm sorry I lost my wife. Neither of them deserved what was done to'em. I know you loved him. I loved her. But the love I always had for you was still in there down deep. It never went away, and that is why it came back to the top so quick."

"I know. I feel the same way. It was a great tragedy, too great to endure almost. But we found each other now. We have each other to hang onto. And because of that we can go on living."

"Yeah," he said. "That's true. We can go on."

"Got your coffee," the waitress said. "Know what you want to eat?"

"Uh, give us a minute," Sullivan said.

"Sure. Just wave at me."

"I tried to find you, but you had already left the ranch."

"Yes, of course. I didn't know what happened to your wife. When I came here, I inquired about you with the Rangers. They told me what happened."

"Yeah, I didn't know you were here, so I went off to south Texas on a job. Soon as I got back, I was sent to El Paso, where I am stationed now. I'm just over here trying to recruit some new men. We lost half of ours over there fightin' bad men."

"What happened to her?"

"Don't know if you want to know. But you asked. I'll tell ya."

"Ready now?" the waitress asked.

"Uh, oh, steaks all right?" he asked Constance.

"That's fine," she replied.

"Yeah, steaks, potatoes, bread, beans."

"Coming out soon."

Sullivan picked up his coffee and drank two sips of it. He wondered how much he ought to tell Constance about what happened.

"There was a killer who wanted to get even with me because I had killed many of his Indian friends. He was a breed. He came to our house, killed the Sheriff down stairs and took her away. I was in the barn. We had laid a trap for him, we thought. I finally went in the house and found the Sheriff dead, and her missin'. He took her to the ranch, and, well, sliced her open Indian style. I'll not say more. He wanted to draw me out to follow him so he could kill me. To make a short story no longer than it ought to be, I killed him, the long and the short of it.

"I had been a deputy in town, ya know, tryin' to get away from the Rangers so we could have some kind of life nearly normal, whatever that is, but all that drew me back into the Rangers. Here I am."

"I'm so sorry you went through all of that."

"Yeah. But you had your own heartbreak, and I was there when it happened."

"It was not our fault."

"No. It just was, that's all."

Constance looked at him for a couple of moments, and then she asked him a question.

"What are we going to do about us?"

"Why, we'll get married, of course. If you'll have me."

"Sure I will. I married you once already. Nothing has changed about that."

"Where and when?"

"That's the Methodist Church you came by at the school. I go there. I know the preacher. He will do it for us."

"We'll move your stuff in my room after we eat. Get married tomorrow, if we can that quick."

"I'm sure we can."

"We won't tell him you're already in my room."

"What he don't know will not hurt us."

After a few more minutes, the waitress came back with the food. She put the plates on the table.

"More coffee?"

"Sure," Sullivan said.

Chapter Eighteen

As they stood in the living room of the parsonage, the Methodist preacher, Reverend Robert Byington, smiled at them.

"You may kiss your bride," he said.

His wife was standing there behind Constance. She put her hankey to her face and wiped away a tear.

Betsy Mae Carington, the other teacher, smiled and hugged Constance.

It was late Friday afternoon. The happy couple would have

the weekend alone.

Claudia Byington had hurriedly made a cake for them. She handed Constance a large knife so she and Sullivan together could cut the cake. Then she placed slices on little plates and gave one to each person. She poured everyone a cup of coffee.

Sullivan slipped Reverend Byington two dollars.

"Thanks, Preacher. Appreciate it very much."

"You are quite welcomed."

Then they all went to the hotel dining room for a celebration dinner, which Sullivan paid for.

After everyone else had left, Sullivan looked over at Constance as they sat back down at the table.

"We got some big decisions to make," he said.

"I know."

"I am stationed days and days away at El Paso."

"And I have my job here."

"I can't just quit without completing what I came here to do, and leave my men over there high and dry. I don't know how long I'll have to stay there. We've been given a job to do there, and I feel obligated. The Rangers been good to me."

"I understand completely," she replied. "And I can't leave Betsy Mae high and dry with both classes."

"I know. I won't be goin' back till I can get at least five new men. I don't know how long that will take. Could be soon. Could be drawn out. I don't know."

"So what does all this mean?" she asked.

"I think we both know, don't we?"

"Yes."

"I ain't at all sure I would want you makin' that long trip through all that hostile territory any way. It's dangerous country. And El Paso ain't like here in Austin."

"I would do it for you."

"I know you would, but I would not want you to do that. I guess I'm sayin', and we're both sayin', I go back when I have to and you stay here till I can get back.

When I am done over there, I'll talk to my boss, Major Pendergrass, and see if I can get put some place more civilized, like back up around Dallas maybe."

"That would be good."

"This is a dangerous job I have, ya know. Anything can happen anywhere anytime. I know it is unfair to you to be married to me because I could go out and just not come back."

"I know that, but that could be true of anything you do, being a deputy in a town, raising cattle, owning a store. It's just a dangerous time in a dangerous part of this country."

"Yeah, I know you're right about that. What if we have another child?"

"We'll worry about that when and if it happens."

"I know. It's just that I lost you once, and now we have another chance at being together. I just hope it goes better this time."

"Sure. It will all work out, I know."

"Yeah. Work out. Well, let's go home."

They left the dining room and retired to their home in room two eleven.

The next day, they walked around town and looked in stores and shops. Sullivan bought Constance two new dresses and a new pair of shoes. He bought himself a new pair of boots.

On the doors and windows of many stores, they saw the posters Pendergrass had put in place advertising for new recruits for the Texas Rangers. They stopped to look at one of them.

"Do you think these will do any good?" Constance asked.

"I sure do hope so. I hope we can get some good men. If not, and if this drags out a long time, then I will just have to stay here with you and try to be a normal husband. I might never get back to El Paso."

"Oh, that would be a terrible development. I guess we could just try to adjust, and make the most of it."

"Think we could do that?" he asked.

"I don't know, but I am willing to try."

Chapter Nineteen

On Monday morning, Sullivan went to the Ranger office after Constance left to go to school.

"Come in Sullivan. Have a seat," Major Pendergrass said without even looking up. He continued looking through a small stack of papers. Finally, he turned his attention to Sullivan.

"How's the married man today?"

"I'm fine."

"Being married is a hard thing sometime for a Ranger and for

his wife."

"Yes, Sir. We know that very well."

"I've seen it work, and I've seen it not work."

"Yeah. Speakin' of work. Anybody wantin' any work, as a Ranger that is?"

"Not one living soul. Not yet."

There was a knock on the door to Pendergrass's office.

"Come!"

Pat Cline, the young Ranger at the front desk, stuck his head in and spoke.

"Sir, there's a young man here inquiring."

"About what?"

"About being a Texas Ranger."

Pendergrass looked at Sullivan, his face lit up and his eyes widened.

"Show the gentleman in, show him in."

The young man came through the door. He was six feet tall, weighed around one hundred and seventy or eighty pounds. He had red hair, a big smile, a gleam in his eyes.

Pendergrass walked around his desk to shake his hand.

"I'm Major Pendergrass. This is Captain Toombs Sullivan. He's stationed over at El Paso, and he needs some men. Sit down, sit down."

When all three of them were seated, Pendergrass looked at the young man intently.

"What's your name?"

"George Bailey."

"George Bailey. Where are you from George Bailey?"

"I'm from Georgia."

"Sullivan here is from Georgia. Half the state must have moved out here. What part of Georgia?"

"A town named Vienna, down below Macon."

"Vienna? Kinda like in Austria."

"Not really."

"Sullivan is from up near Chattanooga. Were you in the war?"

"No, Sir. I was too young."

"Just how old are you?"

"I'll be twenty-one in three months."

"So, you are twenty."

"Yes, Sir."

"What makes you want to be a Ranger?"

"I need a job. You need men."

"How did you grow up?"

"In town. My father owned a store. I worked there a lot growing up. With the war the store finally closed. The slaves were free. Not enough of them stayed on to pick cotton and other crops. The town had a hard time, my father too. The economy there hit bottom. My folks are gone on now. Nothing there to keep me. So I came out here. I heard there were many good opportunities here, for what I did not know. I never thought about being a lawman before. But I was raised right. Grew up in the Methodist Church. I believe in doing what is right, and I don't like wrong-doing and those who do it. If you want that kind of man, then I am your man."

"You handle weapons?"

"Oh, yes. I've been hunting everything in Georgia since I was about nine years old."

"Got a rifle?"

"No, Sir."

"Got a pistol?"

George Bailey stood up, pulled back his coat on the right side, and revealed a high holster at his waist containing a pistol. He sat back down.

"Got a horse?"

"Yes, Sir. Bought him in Dallas. Came to Texas on the train.

Been around horses most all my life."

"You think you can do this?"

"Yes, Sir. That's why I came in here."

"What do you think, Sullivan?"

"Swear the man in and give him a badge."

"Stand up and raise your right hand."

George Bailey stood up and looked closely at Pendergrass.

"Do you swear to uphold the laws of the United States of America and the State of Texas, and do all you can to protect the lives of our citizens, so help you God."

"I do."

Pendergrass reached in a drawer, pulled out a badge, walked around the desk and pinned it on Texas Ranger George Bailey. He then shook his hand.

Sullivan stepped over, shook his hand, and spoke to him.

"Congratulations."

"There's a big trash can out there in the office. On your way out throw that hat of yours in it. Sullivan, take this Ranger over to the store and make him look like one, and get him a rifle too."

"Yes, Sir."

Chapter Twenty

Toombs Sullivan and George Bailey stepped onto the boardwalk in front of the Texas Ranger office. Bailey was bare-headed.

"Nothing wrong with yore hat. It just wasn't big enough. As you can see, we wear wide-brimmed hats. Without them we would all burn up. Come on with me."

They walked across the street and down two blocks. They came to a large general store. They stepped inside, and Sullivan pointed off to the left at several shelves of hats.

George Bailey began trying some of them on.

"Oh, I like this one."

"Nope," Sullivan said. "This one. Put it on."

Bailey put the hat on his head and looked toward Sullivan.

"That's the one, George. Follow me."

They walked further down the left side of the store. They passed a shelf with scarves on it. Sullivan picked up a blue and white one, and handed it to Bailey.

"Here."

They came to a place where there were vests and short coats.

"Pick one of each and put them on."

"I don't have money for all this."

"You don't need money for all this. The state of Texas has money for all this. Just do it."

After Bailey had the vest and the coat on, Sullivan looked at him.

"Good. Let me see your boots."

Bailey pulled up his pants leg.

"No. Follow me."

Next Sullivan found for Bailey calf-high boots, chaps, two pairs of pants, and two shirts. They stepped over to the counter. The owner of the store was Shelby Sangster.

"Mister Sangster," said Sullivan, "this man needs one of those Winchesters right there."

Sangster handed a rifle over to Bailey,

"That is called a Yellow Boy. See the brass housing there."

Turning from Bailey back to Sangster, Sullivan said, "And two boxes of cartridges. Put all this on the Texas Ranger account."

"Sure. Glad to."

"Bailey, the people we will face have this same rifle, and only God knows what else."

"Oh."

"Let's gather all this up, and then go get you a room at the hotel we use. You'll have to share it with whoever the next man is who joins us."

"Fine."

They walked back up the street, crossed it, and went in the hotel used by the Rangers.

The desk clerk on duty was Baldy Jones, a man Sullivan knew fairly well.

"Baldy, how ya doin'?"

"Fine, Mister Sullivan. You?"

"I am good."

"Glad to hear about the wedding goings on. I was off duty a few days. Best wishes."

"Thanks. This is George Bailey, a new Ranger. He needs a room. The next new man will room with him. You got rooms for four more men, two per room?"

"I do."

"Save'em then."

Baldy handed George Bailey the key.

"It's room two thirteen."

They went upstairs and put Bailey's things in the room.

"You got more stuff someplace?" Sullivan asked.

"Yes, Sir. A flop house about five blocks south."

"Go get ya stuff. I'll be at the office if ya have questions about anything. We eat most of our meals in the dining room downstairs. Sometime we go over to the saloon across the street. The Rangers pay for meals here and also our rooms. Anything we eat anywhere else you pay for it. And don't call me Sir. Just Sullivan."

"Yes, Sir, I mean sure, Sullivan."

"Good."

Sullivan left the hotel and went back to the office. He went in to talk with Pendergrass.

"I got Bailey taken care of. I think he'll be a good man. Now I'd like to get five more. That'd give us six new ones. I hope we can get this done soon and get on to El Paso. Time is wastin'"

"I wouldn't say it's wasting. You got married and are on your way to rebuilding your company. Lots of progress seems to me."

"Yeah, I know. But I can only imagine what's happenin' over there is west Texas."

Chapter Twenty-one

"Here's what we're gonna do, Men," said Jack the Beast Stalker. "Well, first, where's a place we never hit?"

"Dallas," answered Pete de Luca.

"You must be a genius, you idiot. Of course, we never hit Dallas. I'm talkin' about here where we are. Anybody else got a bright idea?"

"Fort Worth?" asked Markus Grassa.

"I ought to shoot both of you right here right now."

Angelo Alvarez raised his hand, and said "El Paso."

"Yes! Now here is a man after my own heart. El Paso.

Guess what they got in El Paso? You two keep quiet. What Angelo?"

"A bank."

"Now what is in a bank, Pete?"

"Money."

"You just saved your own life and kept me from killing you. Money! What are we gonna do about that money, Markus?"

"We are going to get that money. Make a withdrawal."

"Yes, we are."

Stalker's forty-five men were seated in a circle around a campfire. He looked at them for a few moments.

"Here is the plan. We go in tomorrow. Ten of you, led by Angelo, will hit that bank. Get the money. Shoot up the town. Make lots of noise. Then get out of town. Run for the river and go across. The cavalry will rush out to the rescue. As soon as they leave the fort, thirty-five of you and me will rush the fort. They have money there in the office and all the supplies we need. Five of you will get a wagon. Load it up, then get out of there. By the time the cavalry sees what is happening, as they stand at the river, we will all be gone. Zed, you and Moss kill the guards at the gate as we go in. Jacob, Pede, kill the guards at the office building. You four go in first. Lonzo, pick ten men and wait at the gate for the cavalry to come rushing back. Cut them down before they can get to us. Now get some sleep."

The next morning, at a little after nine, Angelo Alvarez and nine raiders quietly rode into El Paso. They stopped in front of the bank. Eight of them dismounted while two stayed with the horses. The eight men entered the bank.

"Everybody on the floor!" screamed out Alvarez.

Two clerks, one bank president, and four customers, three men and a woman, quickly laid down on the floor.

"Get the money! Fast!"

The raiders filled several bags with the cash they could find, both from behind the counter and from the open bank vault.

Then they went outside and got on their horses. They began firing their pistols in the air and at store windows. They rode up and down the street.

Pow!

Pow!

Pow!

Pow!

A bugle sounded inside of Fort Bliss!

"Get ready, Boys," said Jack the Beast, as they hid in a grove of trees near the fort.

They heard orders being given inside the fort. In a few minutes, they clearly heard Colonel Kicklighter.

"Mount up! Forward! At the gallop, charge!"

The cavalry came roaring out of the gate headed for El Paso.

When they were far down the road, Jack the Beast turned to his men.

"All right. Here we go."

The raiders charged the fort!

The guards at the gate were shot dead!

The guards at the office building were shot dead!

Shots rang out all over the fort!

Pow!

Pow!

Pow!

Jack the Beast and his men rushed into the office building!

They took the payroll and other money while a wagon was loaded with food and weapons and ammunition!

Then the wagon went out of the fort and headed south with Jack the Beast and his men right behind it!

The cavalry reached the city of El Paso!

They saw the bank robbers at the far end of the main street!

They charged after them!

But the raiders headed for the river and were across it in no time at all!

Three Texas Rangers heard the disturbance and went to the door of the saloon to look out and see what was happening. It was puzzling to them.

Ranger Corporal Timothy Davis said, "My, my."

Marshall Ted Wheeler was standing in the edge of the river with his boots off. He had heard the shots, but knew Deputy Sam Fears could handle a couple of drunks firing their pistols in the air. It was Wheeler's day off and he was trying to catch some fish. He was astonished to suddenly see ten men on horseback come speeding by him.

Colonel Kicklighter held up his hand, halting his men! He thought he heard the shots back the fort!

"The fort!" he cried out. He turned his horse around and yelled out.

"Charge!"

Back to the fort they raced as fast as they could!

As they drew near the fort shots rang out!

Pow!

Pow!

Bang!

Bang!

Pow!

They were being fired upon by someone at the fort!

"Follow me!" Kicklighter shouted, as he quickly turned left to go around the fort!

Three cavalrymen fell dead from their horses!

When the cavalry was out of sight, the raiders at the fort hopped on their horses and left!

Kicklighter and his men went in a back gate, knowing they could save that situation.

It was too late.

Chapter Twenty-two

George Bailey, looking like a Texas Ranger, was sitting in the office with Major Pendergrass and Toombs Sullivan.

There was a knock at the door.

"Major, there's a young man here who wants to speak to you,"

said Pat Cline.

"Show him in," Pendergrass said, as he stood up.

Sullivan and Bailey stood up as well.

A tall lanky young man entered the room.

"Howdy, I'm Slim Dunken. Saw yore ad about hiring."

"Yes, we are. I'm Major Pendergrass. This is Captain Toombs Sullivan and Ranger Donald Bailey. Pull up a chair and have a seat."

After they were seated, Pendergrass asked Duncan to speak.

"Tell us about yourself. Where ya from, all that."

"Well, Sir, I come from South Carolina. I was in the war. That's where I grew up, I guess. You either grow up or die in the war, ya know. I been making my way here since the war ended. I'd work at a place, get a little money, moved on till I could stop and work somewhere else. Worked on farms mostly. Farm workers are needed badly everywhere. It was always my dream to come to Texas. Well, I saw a notice about you Rangers needing men. I am one. Here I am."

"Good with weapons?"

"Oh, yea. I survived the war."

"Nough said. Got a horse?"

"Yes, Sir. A good one."

"You see how Ranger Bailey is dressed?"

"Yes, Sir."

"That's how you need to dress. Stand up. Raise ya right hand. Do you promise to obey and enforce the laws of the United States of America and the State of Texas, so help you God?"

"I do."

"Congratulations. You are now a Texas Ranger."

Pendergrass moved around the desk, pinned the badge on him, and shook his hand. Then Sullivan and Bailey also shook his hand.

"Captain, this man needs to be outfitted."

"Sure. Bailey, why don't you take this Ranger across the street and outfit him. Get him a Yellow Boy too."

"Yes, Sir, uh, Sullivan."

Four more men came in that morning. They were each interviewed, accepted, and sworn in. All of them said they were good with weapons and had a good horse.

Ted Kite was from Virginia. He looked to be about forty years old. He had fought with General Robert E. Lee and was proud of it. He was medium height, rather thin looking, dark complexion, and had a two-week growth of facial hair.

Roger Maples was from Atlanta, Georgia. He too was a veteran of the war. He said he was in a Georgia cavalry unit and had chased General Sherman all over the state. At the time he wanted to kill him because of what he was doing, but, he said, the war is over and all that was behind him now. He thought he would make a good Ranger because of his sense of right and wrong.

Ronald Wildman was from the great State of Mississippi. His father had a cotton farm, but that was all gone now. So was his family. His mother died of consumption. His father died of a

broken heart. He said he had the right last name because he could be a wild man when he needed to be.

Clem Young was nineteen years old. He was short and thin, stringy hair hung from under his hat. When he took the hat off, his brown hair fell across his face and ears. He grew up in Texas on his father's ranch. He came in from a trip to the store in town and found his family dead and all the cattle and horses gone. He had a lot of reasons for wanting to be a Ranger, and that was one of them. He said a little revenge never hurt nobody but the one on the receiving end and he deserved it.

Sullivan and Bailey spent the rest of that day outfitting the new Rangers. They also got them settled in rooms at the hotel and their horses housed at the livery stable the Rangers used.

Now Sullivan had what he had come back to Austin to get. He also had married Constance, something he had not counted on at all. Now instead of everything being simple, everything was complicated. But he and Constance had talked it through. They understood how things were and how they had to be for now. That did not make it any easier.

Sullivan went back to the office in late afternoon. When he walked into Pendergrass's office, he saw a somber look on his face.

"You better have a seat," Pendergrass said.

Sullivan sat down across from Pendergrass, who handed him a telegram.

"Read this."

Sullivan looked down at it and began reading.

El Paso hit by Stalker raiders Stop Bank robbed and

Fort Bliss robbed Stop Money stolen from both and

supplies from fort Stop Three soldiers killed Stop

Timothy Davis

Sullivan looked up at Pendergrass, but did not seem all that shocked.

"Well, I had planned on doing a little work with the new men before we left. That idea just got blown away. We'll get as soon as we can."

"Good. And God-speed."

Chapter Twenty-three

Sullivan and Constance sat at the table, having finished their evening meal. They both were drinking coffee.

"I have some bad news," he said.

"You're leaving. Right away."

"How did you know?"

"I could tell just by looking at you. I could see it in your eyes."

"That bad, eh?"

"Yes. Tell me about it."

"We got a gang of raiders over at El Paso. They did something new this time. They came into town and robbed the bank and also Fort Bliss. Stole money from both. Three soldiers were killed. That's really all I know. But we have to go. Those six men I introduced you to a while ago are, like I said, our new Rangers. I'll have to take them over there and put a stop to that wild gang. They ravage the land and the people. Now the town and the fort."

"I know you have to do it. Would it do any good for me to say, be careful?"

"Yes. In a way. Maybe. I don't know how long this will take. It could be weeks. Maybe months. I don't know."

"I will be here, of course, waiting for your safe return and praying for that."

"Thanks. I know it."

Sullivan looked at Constance. Then he looked at the men seated near them. He looked back at her.

"I need to talk to them. Then I'll be upstairs."

"I'll begin getting your things together."

"Thanks. I'll be along."

He watched her as she got up and left the room. Then he moved over to the men and took a chair.

"You Boys enjoy your meal?"

"Oh, yea."

"Sure did."

"It was great."

Others nodded their heads in agreement.

"I'm glad you did," Sullivan said. "It'll be the last good one until we get to El Paso. We're pulling out of here in the morning. I was hoping to have a couple of days to talk with you all and give you the ins and outs of being a Ranger. But we got a problem."

Sullivan then told them all about the raid on El Paso and Fort Bliss. He told them about Jack the Beast Stalker and his gang.

"I've never seen him, nor has anyone else and lived to tell us what he looks like. We don't know much about his raiders except that he has a big gang. We think it is made up of whites, Mexicans, half-breeds, some Indians probably.

"He is a mean ruthless killer and they are made in his image. They have raided ranches the way Comanches do. They kill everybody there, sometime take females captive, steal cattle and horses, trade with Indians, burn down everything.

"We'll be up against Comanches too. They are different, a different kind of Indian. Apaches jump off their horses and fight on the ground. We fight them too, by the way. Comanches are maybe the finest horsemen in the world. They are the only Indians that fight on horseback. They can shoot guns and arrows while riding full out. They often take females to be their wives. They will sometime take children to raise as their own. At other times, they'll kill everybody at a place they raid, women and children.

"But they ain't our first concern. We may run into them and have to fight them, but the first thing we got to do is stop Jack the Beast.

"We'll spend a lot of time camped out some place at night. We'll post guards and watch the horses closely. Indians like to steal horse, especially at night. They will kill you so they can get a horse or two. Ya have to be alert at all times.

"The first responsibility and the mission of the Texas Rangers is to protect settlers and ranchers and farmers from Indians and raiders like that gang. We put our lives in danger to do that.

"You still want to be a Texas Ranger?"

Most of them smiled and a few of them laughed.

"It's what we signed on for," said George Bailey.

"We knew it weren't no picnic," said Ted Kite.

"Well, the fact that you had vacancies told us something,"

commented Clem Young.

"I guess my secret is out," Sullivan responded. "We've had five men over there killed. You're taking their places.

"Check your gear tonight, everything you wanna take with you. We'll be up at dawn, eat quick, and be gone.

"Bailey, you and whoever you pick will be in charge of the two mules we're taking. Get some others to help y'all load up all the supplies.

"Questions anybody?

"Get some good sleep tonight. We got a long journey ahead of us."

The men filed out and headed upstairs.

Sullivan headed upstairs to room two eleven.

Chapter Twenty-four

"You will write, right?" asked Constance.

"Right."

"Always be careful."

"Careful."

"Don't take any chances."

"Wrong."

"Why would you?"

"Every day I go out the door I will be taking a chance."

"I know but . . . ."

"My middle name is Chance. I am a Texas Ranger. That's it."

Constance walked with Sullivan downstairs to the street where the men were waiting with the horses and the two pack mules which held everything they would need for the trip.

He put his saddle bags on his horse and tied them down. Then he came back up on the boardwalk and kissed her.

He got on his horse and looked at her one last time. He could not believe he was leaving her, but he was.

He turned his horse's head to the west.

"Let's go, Men."

They rode slowly out of Austin headed not only to El Paso, but to an uncertain future that was coming to them very quickly.

They made close to forty miles that day. Then they stopped near a creek for the night. It was a good place to water the horses and mules and have water for themselves.

Sullivan posted guards after supper. He slept very little, knowing it was the first time they had done that. He wanted to be sure they stayed awake and alert.

The first day and the first night had both been uneventful. He was thankful for that.

Every day and every night was the same on their journey. They made good time during the day and were not disturbed during the night.

Sullivan thought it was too uneventful. But nothing ever happened.

They pulled into El Paso late one afternoon. It was a Saturday.

They went straight to the livery stable, unloaded their gear, put up their saddles, stored everything that was still left on the mules, and went to their hotel.

Sullivan checked them all into the hotel. While he was doing that, Boyd came in the lobby.

"Hello, Sullivan. Good trip?"

Sullivan turned around and shook his hand.

"Looks like my trip was better than your stay."

"I hope it was. I know the meaning of the word surprise now."

"Let me put my stuff in my room, and you can tell me about it. I'll tell you about the new men."

Sullivan put his saddlebags, bedroll, and rifles in his room, and came back down to the dining room.

He and Boyd sat at a table in a far back corner. The new men began drifting in.

"What happened here?"

"It was the Stalker gang. They pulled off the perfect raid. They hit the bank, drew the army out, and when the army got here, they hit the fort."

"And where did they go?"

"They went south along the river I assume. What I was told, though I, of course, did not see them."

"Where was Marshall Wheeler?"

"He was fishing, I was told."

"Did he catch anything?"

"I was not told that."

"Did he go after them?"

"Of course not."

"Didn't think he had."

"Nope."

"We'll have to, ya know."

"Yep."

"Better let the new men rest a day or so."

"Good idea."

"I need to rest too."

"Figured."

"I think we got some good men. You'll like them fine I believe."

"I'm sure I will. If you say they are good, they are good."

"They are good."

"Any news from Austin?"

"I not only got new men in Austin, I got something else as well."

"What would that be?"

"I got a new wife."

"Got a what?"

"A new wife. Well, my first wife, like new. She was in Austin waiting on me. She knew I would show up there at some point. I did."

"Well, that is wonderful. Glad y'all could get back together."

"Yeah. Life takes some funny turns, and some of them ain't funny at all."

"I might take me a wife some day."

"I recommend it."

"You would know."

"All the new men are in here now. Come on. I'll introduce you."

Chapter Twenty-five

The next morning at breakfast the new men were meeting Tim Davis, Charley Easom, and Eddie Canton.

Sullivan tapped his spoon on his coffee cup.

"Hate to interrupt, but time for an announcement. Now that y'all have all met each other, it's time to look at what we are goin' to do.

"For our new Rangers, I want to tell you there is a gang of raiders we been trying to stop. Jack the Beast Stalker is their leader. They been robbin' and killin' ranchers and farmers. They'll burn everything down, steal the stock, trade or sell to Indians and Comancheros. They're getting' bolder. While I was in Austin, they came in here and robbed the bank. The army came out to help, and when they did, the raiders hit the fort, Fort Bliss, just up the road, and stole money and supplies.

"We're goin' after them. It falls to us. Nobody else. It's what our job is. We're goin' out in the morning.

"Their trail is cold now, of course. Won't even be any tracks left. They went south along down the river. But I been down that way before chasin' Indians and bad men. That was before there was any Rangers here. I was out of Dallas then. Well, we're goin'.

"Now today we got work to do, but not much. Rest as much as you can. Get yore gear ready, weapons cleaned, all that.

"We got supplies to pack for the mules. We got four now. We'll take all four.

"Boyd and Davis will be in charge of gettin' everything we need ready, and gettin' the mules ready. They'll tell you what you need to do to help them. You'll take turns leadin' the mules once we are out.

"Any questions?"

"I got one," said Clem Young. "How long you think we'll be out on this trip?"

"Not to give ya a short answer, but until we come back, we kill them or they kill us. If they kill us, we ain't comin' back."

"Thanks. I think."

"Anything else?"

Sullivan paused a minute, looked around at all of them.

"All right. Let's get to it."

The Rangers got up from the tables and left the room.

Sullivan stayed where he was and sat back down. He had a lot to think about, mainly two things – how to stop the raiders and how to keep his men alive. He wondered if the first was possible without the second being impossible. Most of them were young and would be facing some things they had never seen before. But he had been through it when he was younger. They would grow up, learn from it, or die. It was not up to him. It was up to fate or their destiny or God or luck or whatever ya want to call what happens in life to any and every man. He waved at the waitress.

"Coffee, please?"

She came over to his table with a pot of coffee. The steam was rising from the pot. Then the steam was rising from the coffee in his cup.

"Thanks."

She walked away as Sullivan poured his coffee in his saucer and blew it. He held the saucer up and sipped the coffee.

When he was through with the coffee, he went up to his room.

He decided to do what he had told the men to do. He first cleaned his pistol. Then he cleaned his Winchester Yellow Boy, and next his Sharps. He cleaned the dust off his boots. He took the clothes he had worn on the trip from Austin downstairs and asked the desk clerk to get them cleaned and back to him by late afternoon.

Next, he left the hotel and went to the livery stable. He wanted to check on his horse and clean his saddle. When he got there, Boyd was looking at the mules.

"How ya think these Boys will do?" he asked Boyd.

"Oh, all right I would say. We'll find out. That's for sure."

"Yeah. I'm just worried about this trip. I don't know why, but I have this bad feelin'. I never did before anywhere I ever went. I just did it, faced it, did what I had to do, ya know."

"Well, we'll know soon enough how they gonna be. Once we get to where we're goin' and face whoever we find, we'll see what happens. Protect them as we can, but they'll have to take their chances just as we will."

"Yeah, I know. So none of ya'll saw Stalker?"

"No. There was shootin' in the street. That was all we know. Happened so fast. He was at the fort I guess with the bigger group."

"The man is smart. Maybe one of the smartest I ever come up against."

Boyd looked at Sullivan a moment. Then he smiled.

"He ain't as smart as we are."

Chapter Twenty-six

The next morning, the Texas Rangers stationed at El Paso, pulled out of the town and headed south-east along the Rio Grande River, the grandest river of all for those people who lived in that part of Texas.

"Davis take the point," Sullivan said.

At the end of that first day, they stopped to make camp alongside the river. There was a routine that had to be followed. The veterans knew it well, but the new men would have

to learn it. It would be the same every night.

First, they had to water the animals. They lined up along the river and let the horses and mules drink as much as they wanted. Taking care of them was primary. The men dismounted and filled their canteens. Some of them knelt down and drank from the river. The importance of water could not be overstated. Water is life. No water, no life.

Then they strung a long rope between two trees. They unsaddled their horses and unpacked the mules. They tied the horses and mules to the rope.

They gathered wood to makes three fires. They put their saddles near the campfires.

They set up three portable tables. Those who knew cooking got their meal started. They had large slabs of bacon, cans of beans, made corn fritters, and started coffee boiling.

Soon they were eating their supper, sitting on the ground or stumps and logs or large boulders.

Sullivan was the last man in line. He walked over to Boyd and sat down on a fallen tree. After taking a few bites, he spoke to him.

"You post the guards. You and Davis look after them. Use the new men tonight. No danger tonight, I would not think. Would not want to start them out further along in more hostile territory."

"Yeah, you're right. We'll see to it."

"What are you thinking about where we're headed?"

"I don't know. You know this area of the state better than I do. I never been in these parts before."

"I never been where I bet they are headed, but I been in this side of the state before chasin' Indians and bad men."

"You catch'em?" Boyd asked.

"You know I did. Killed'em too. Killed'em dead."

"Best kind of killin'."

"I think so. Well, I think our raiders are headed to the Quitman Mountains."

"Never heard of that."

"Named after John Quitman. He was some lawyer from Mississippi who raised a militia and fought in the Mexican War. He discovered that area. Sam Houston offered him some big position in his army, but he said no. He went back home and became governor of Mississippi. They're west of Sierra Blanca, those Quitman Mountains."

Boyd had a questioning look on his face.

"Sierra Blanca. White mountains. Lots of white flowers all over the place. Good place to hide out too. We could have a problem if that's where they've gone. Either place."

"I would expect nothin' else, want nothin' less."

Sullivan smiled at him.

After supper was finished, Boyd placed the guards, one at each end of their camp. He started with George Bailey and Slim Dunken. They would be followed by Clem Young and Ted Kite. Then it would be Ronald Wildman and Roger Maples.

Boyd and Tim Davis would rotate checking on them, making sure there was no problem. There was always the possibility that Indians could sneak into camp and steal horses. Boyd and Sullivan had experienced a lot of that. This made them cautious, sometime overly cautious.

Sullivan sat by the fire where his saddle was near. Sleeping on a journey like this one was always a problem for him. He thought about Constance, wondered how she was doing.

Finally, he laid down and dozed off.

Not long after midnight, someone touched his shoulder. He opened his eyes. It was Boyd.

Boyd cocked his head toward the north, motioning in that direction. He put his finger up to his lips, and then whispered.

"We may have a visitor."

Sullivan slowly and quietly got up. He picked up his pistol.

"Show me," he whispered.

He then followed Boyd as they slipped through the camp. Soon they reached the horses.

Clem Young saw them coming. He pointed just to the other side of where the horses were tied. Then he held up three fingers and pointed again.

Sullivan sent Young up along the river, Boyd straight at the horses, and he went around to the right.

They crept along, stopping, listening, looking, then taking a few more steps.

Each of them stood for a long time waiting. But they did not see anything. Finally, they decided they must have left.

When they met back together again, Sullivan shook his head.

"I guess they gave up. Must have seen us or heard us."

"I swear I heard somebody over there," said Clem Young.

"I don't doubt that one bit," Sullivan responded.

"They were just feelin' us out, wantin' to know how many of us and how many horses we have," Boyd suggested.

"Most likely Comanche," Sullivan replied. "They're the ones, Clem, that are horse crazy. They'll do anything to get horses. Anything. Even risk death to get'em. I am always glad to oblige."

Sullivan went back to his bedroll. He laid down and looked up. The stars were always there. Never failed.

Though he had gone to sleep, he was wide awake now. That was it for the night most likely. No more sleep.

Th next morning, the Rangers were busy breaking camp. They put the tables and all of their supplies on the mules. Their personal gear they put on their horses after they saddled them.

Boyd got Sullivan's attention. He walked over to where Boyd was standing beyond where the horses were.

"Look at the ground," Boyd said.

"Yeah. Can't tell for sure, but must have been at least three, maybe four, five."

"Comanches."

"No doubt."

"We were lucky."

"Yep," Sullivan replied. "Wonder what changed their minds?"

"Maybe they didn't change them."

"Be with us until, right?"

"Afraid so," Boyd answered.

"All right, Boys," Sullivan called out, "let's get goin'!"

Chapter Twenty-seven

"Eddie Canton, take the point!" Sullivan said.

Canton rode on ahead of the company, as they mounted up and left their camp.

Sullivan was leading in front. Boyd was back behind everyone else, keeping an eye out just in case.

After a little over an hour, Boyd passed by the others and came along beside Sullivan.

"Guess what," Boyd said.

"Don't tell me."

"They're back there behind us."

"I said don't tell me."

"Figured you needed to know."

"How many?"

"Can't tell yet."

"Maybe you better find out."

"I'll do it."

Boyd turned his horse around, left the others, and pulled up on a little hill that had a few young trees, just tall enough to conceal him.

He waited a few minutes, then he saw them in the distance.

He tried to count, but he could not see them clearly. It looked like there could be eight or maybe ten or maybe twelve or maybe more or maybe less. The reality was they were being followed by Indians who wanted their horses. And they would kill to have them.

Boyd rode along in the tree line until he went over a little rise. Then he got back on the trail and soon caught up with the Rangers.

"Must be between eight and ten, twelve or more. Couldn't tell," he told Sullivan. "They got a lone rider out ahead of'em sizin' things up the way we do."

"Wonderful. We'll have to deal with them now or later. Today or tonight. What say you?"

"I say we get it over with out here in the daylight. We wait till tonight we are shootin' in the dark," Boyd replied.

"Just what I was thinkin'."

Sullivan held up his hand and stopped the others.

"Boys, we got a problem. We're bein' followed by those Indians who were snoopin' around last night. They really want our horse, enough to kill us for them. There ain't but one thing to do. We got to deal with them now. Waitin' till later is just puttin' it off. We can't do that. So we kill'em now. I know most of ya never had to do this before. You might not like it. Well, you want to keep yore horse and yore hair? Then kill'em. Boyd's gonna take part of ya down along the river in those trees. The rest of ya come with me up this little hill. We'll hide in those young trees up there. Don't shoot when we first see them. They will send a rider on ahead just a little, like a scout. Then the rest will come. I'll fire the first shot. Use yore Winchesters at first. If they get close to us and yore rifle get empty, throw it down and use yore pistol. Don't hesitate, don't think, don't delay. Just do it. All right, let's get to it."

Boyd took his group to the river. Sullivan took his men up the little hill. Both groups disappeared into the trees.

The Rangers sat on their horses waiting.

Sullivan knew waiting was always the worst part. It gave a man time to think, too much time, too much thinking. Waiting and thinking caused a man to tense up, to get nervous, to have the muscles tighten up. And that was not good. Not good at all. But they could not do anything about that. They had to wait, had to think, had to maybe get ready, ready to kill.

How far back were they? Sullivan wondered.

The seconds were ticking by and the minutes were passing by, but all of them were far too slow. Too many of them were going by. And Sullivan knew it.

What was it? Where were they? Why aren't they here yet?

Sullivan realized something was wrong. The Indians, most likely Comanches, certainly Comanches, were on to them. They knew what the Rangers were doing. They must have had more than one scout out observing them.

No way to get word to Boyd about that, but he surely knew it also. What to do now?

Nothing. Nothing to do but wait, and let them make the first move.

But what would it be? What would they do?

Twenty minutes had come and gone, and there were no Indians, not where they could see them. But they were somewhere. Where?

Sullivan wanted to get word to Boyd. But that was impossible.

He got down off his horse and walked over a few steps so he could peep through the tress. He hoped he would see them, but there was no one there. No one at all.

Chapter Twenty-eight

Where were those Indians? Sullivan kept thinking. They've got to be somewhere near us. Maybe too near us, he thought.

Suddenly shots were being fired down by the river!

Pow!

Pow!

Bang!

Pow!

Bang!

Bang!

"They're in trouble!" Sullivan yelled out.

The Indians had crossed the river and come up behind Boyd and his men!

"Let's go!"

Suddenly there were shots from the top of the little hill, behind Sullivan and his group!

Bang!

Bang!

Bang!

Bang!

The Indians were firing Winchesters at them!

"Turn and fire!" he yelled.

But at who? They were hiding behind the trees!

"Dismount! Take cover!"

That was their only chance!

The Rangers ducked down behind trees and boulders! They began returning fire!

Bang!

Bang!

Bang!

Bang!

Sullivan knew they could sit there all day doing that. He had to get behind them. It was what he always did, the only way to kill those trying to kill you.

He looked around. One of the Rangers was hit bad. He crawled over to him. It was Clem Young. He rolled him over. He was dead. Blood had come out of the right side of his head.

"Well, that does it," he said. "Keep shootin' at'em. I'm going up there and kill them all. Give me a few minutes then stopped shootin'. Don't shoot me."

Sullivan crawled off to the left, careful to not be seen.

His men kept firing as did the Indians.

Bang!

Bang!

Bang!

Bang!

Bullets were whizzing by in and from both directions! Chips of rocks and splinters from trees were flying everywhere!

Sullivan crawled.

Many shots were heard down by the river!

Bang!

Bang!

Pow!

Pow!

Sullivan crawled.

He had to get up there and stop them, kill them, before they picked off all of his men.

The shots kept being fired!

The chips of rocks flew in the air!

The splinters of trees flew in the air!

Sullivan crawled.

He got beyond where the Indians were and turned up the hill, still crawling.

He got even with them.

Then he got up beyond them, behind them.

Two can play this game, he was thinking.

"I'll play it."

There were seven of them crouched down behind trees and rocks.

He was thirty feet behind them, and they had no idea he was there.

Sullivan stopped crawling. He stood up. He aimed his Winchester at the one on his far right. He fired.

Bang!

He charged forward down the hill!

Bang!

Bang!

He dropped his rifle and pulled out his pistol!

Pow!

Pow!

Pow!

Pow!

There was silence, wonderful silence.

And the firing down at the river had ceased. That was either good or bad. Sullivan hope it was good.

He and his men went to the river. There were several dead Comanches lying around.

"You lose any men?" he asked Boyd.

"No. Just lucky, I guess. We got us a live one over here. Several got away back across the river. We killed five of'em."

"We lost Clem."

"Sorry. A good man."

"Show me ya live one."

Chapter Twenty-nine

Boyd led Sullivan over to a Comanche who was seated near the water and was tied up.

"He speaks English," Boyd said.

"What's yore name?" Sullivan asked.

"Eagle that can fly high. Flying Eagle to you whites."

"All right, Flying Eagle. Who are you with? Who is yore big chief? Know you are not alone, you and your dead friends."

"Why tell you?"

Sullivan pulled out his pistol and pointed it at Flying Eagle's head.

"Because I'm goin' to kill you if you don't start talkin'. You no good to us if you can't talk. You better hurry."

"Our band is in Mexico now. Chief is Leaping Mountain Lion. He is big medicine. A great war chief."

"How many warriors, horse thieves ya got?"

"Maybe thirty, forty now."

"You keep all the horses you steal from people like us?"

"Some."

"Some? What you do with the ones you do not keep, along with cattle and women and children who you capture?"

"You ask a lot."

"You better answer a lot. Fast."

"We trade some horses."

"With who?"

"What does that matter?"

"Your life don't matter to me."

"We trade with Stalker. One who stalks at night."

"Where is he now?"

"He is like the wind. He goes where he wills."

"Were you goin' to trade our horses with him?"

"Not my decision."

"Was big war chief Jumping Lion, or whatever you said, goin' to do it, trade them with him?"

"Yes. At right time."

"What time is that?"

"Soon."

"How many head of horses Jumping Lion got?"

"Maybe a hundred horses."

"What does he get for the horses?"

"Many cows."

"Then what? He sells them to our army at our forts, right?"

"You have spoken."

"Where do the horses go?"

"Stalker take them into Mexico. Sell to ranchers."

"Where is that trade gonna take place?"

"Near the mountains."

"Is that where Stalker hides out?"

"I do not know that."

Sullivan moved closer to Flying Eagle and put the pistol six inches from his head.

"He has a camp there. A cabin. Barns. Up the mountain, hidden from view.

"You been there?"

"Yes."

"Which mountains?"

"Name for Quitman soldier."

"Good. You passed the test. You gonna take us there."

"I cannot."

"Then you about to die right here. We ain't taking you along if ya ain't no good to us. Just say it, yes or no."

"Yes."

"Good. Rest a bit. Boyd, send somebody up there to get Clem. We'll bury him here beside the river. A good place for him to sleep."

Boyd sent Bailey and Easom to get Clem Young.

"Somebody find a pony for our friend here to ride," Sullivan said.

In a few minutes, Bailey and Easom came back with Clem Young tied over Bailey's horse.

"We couldn't find his horse. Must'a run off some place," reported Easom.

"Them dead Indians up there didn't get'im. If he don't show up by the time we leave here, he'll just have to find his own way. We ain't got time to go lookin' for him."

Soon a grave was dug for Clem Young in the shade of a tree by the river.

The Rangers gathered around as he was lowered into the ground.

Tim Davis read the Twenty-third Psalm. Boyd said the prayer.

The dirt that had come out of the earth was slowly raked over the body of Clem Young. A make-shift cross was placed at the head of the grave.

The new Rangers stood there looking at the grave. It was something they knew could happen. They had been told about it. But now it was not a story, an opinion, a warning, a caution any longer. It was real now.

Chapter Thirty

"Davis, take the point," Sullivan called out.

Timothy Davis rode on out ahead of the company.

Sullivan and Boyd were riding side by side at the head of the column. Behind them was Flying Eagle with Ted Kite beside him.

"You know what's goin' to happen, don't you?" Boyd asked.

"Yep."

"Those Indians and the raiders are goin' to meet up about

the time we get to them, and we will be in the middle."

"Speck so."

"What are we goin' to do?"

"Don't know yet."

"When you gonna know?"

"We ain't there yet."

"You trust this Indian to lead us right?"

"Haven't thought about it."

"Are you going to think about it?"

"Oh, yeah."

"When?"

"I swear, Boyd, you gettin' like an old woman. Are you all right?"

"I think I'm crazy."

"Let's don't spread that around. Not good for the men."

"Our secret."

At mid-day, they stopped by the river to water the horses, rest, and eat a light meal.

They let the horses drink from the river first.

Then the men did as well, and also filled their canteens.

After a short while, Sullivan called the men together to speak to them.

"Those mountains you see in the distance there are the Quitman Mountains. Off to the left of them is the Sierra Blanca, the White Mountains. They're seven, eight miles away. I never been to either one, but the map says it is so. I reckon it's true. We're goin' to the Quitman Mountains. Our red friend there tells us Jack the Beast has a place in them mountains.

"Them Indians been collectin' horses. The raiders got cattle. They work out some kind of swap. The Indians take the cows to army forts and sell them to the army. I've heard of the army buying back cows with their brand on them that was stolen from them and now they pay for'em again. How the army ever wins any war or battle is beyond me. That's the federal government. But that's a speech for another day.

"The raiders take the horses they get from the Indians and go into Mexico and sell them to big ranchers over there. They get a lot of money that way, I'm sure.

"Now, they all gonna meet up and swap. We don't know when. I hope we get there ahead of them. If we can, we'll set a trap. I don't want to fight the Indians right now, just the raiders. That's who we're after. But we may be fightin' both. Hope not.

"Eat something. Relieve yoreselves while you can. We'll be goin' on right soon."

After ten more minutes, Sullivan called out to the men.

"All right, Boys. Let us be about our father's business. Mount up and let's get at it. Davis, take the point."

They rode toward the mountains, with each man knowing how dangerous this whole thing was going to be. The closer they got to the mountains, the more nervous some of them became, especially the new men. This would be a real test for them. The previous encounter was merely an encounter. This could be a real battle, a shootout the likes of which they had never seen or heard tale of before. But they were Texas Rangers.

This is who they were, and this is what they signed up to do.

Timothy Davis headed for the mountains. Soon he could see the foothills in the distance.

He stopped to look around. He saw some hoof prints, but no fresh sign anywhere.

Davis slowly moved forward, staying close to the tree lines and tall brush and undergrowth as much as he could.

He began thinking there must be a place down here on this level ground where they will meet. Surely, they would not take a large number of horses and cattle up into the hills.

Soon he was at a large open area that might be good for the swap. It was near the river. The ground looked like there had been large numbers of animals grazing there.

Going on further, he came to two corrals. Yes, he thought, one for horses, one for cows. This is the place. And nothing is here yet, no horses, no cows, no Indians, no raiders. We are ahead of them.

Timothy Davis turned his horse around. He had to quickly get back to Sullivan and the Rangers, and let them know what he had found.

He ran his horse as fast as he would go. Soon he saw them.

He pulled up beside Sullivan and stopped.

"Guess what I found."

"Tell me about it."

Chapter Thirty-one

"All right, Boys," Sullivan said to the men, "You heard what Davis said. We've got a chance now to get there before they do. We'll set up an ambush. We'll divide into the same groups we had. My group will be off to the left. We'll find cover of some kind. Boyd and his group will be down along the river. Hide as best as you can. We'll see who gets there first, raiders or Indians. I hope it's the raiders. Likely to be so, since their place is there up in the mountains somewhere. We don't know where the Indians will come from. We'll just have to wait and see. I don't like that part of it, but what can we do? Be alert as we go in. Davis will lead us. Questions? Suggestions?

"All right, let's get to it."

The Rangers mounted up and headed for the mountains.

They rode as fast as they could, determined to get to the staging area before anyone else. They knew that was crucial. If the raiders and the Indians got there before they did, then they would be riding into a confrontation they surely could not win.

Hurry! Hurry! Hurry!

Thirty minutes later, Sullivan held up his hand, halting the company.

"Let's sit here a minute and see what we got."

They all looked around at the level area just before the foothills. There was no one there and there were no fresh tracks from horses, unshod Indians ponies, or cattle. It was a good sign that there was no sign at all.

"Boyd, looks like you got good cover down along the river. And we do as well right over there. I think this is going to work out just right. Take good aim. Make every shot count. Kill'em dead. Take your places, Boys."

Sullivan had Bailey, Canton, Kite, and Wildman. Boyd had with him Davis, Maples, Dunken, and Easom. There were ten men against who knew how many Comanches and raiders. There had to be at least forty or more raiders, and thirty or more Comanches.

Each group went to their assigned area. They were greatly outnumbered, but at times like that for the Rangers, they were always outnumbered. But they had two good things working in their favor. They had good cover. They had the element of surprise. Their enemies, no matter who or how many, would be out in the open, and would have no idea what was about to happen.

Sullivan and his men went up into the rocks and small trees. They hid the horses well. They found their places in little gullies and behind large rocks and boulders. It was good cover, lots of protection, and they would not be seen until they began firing.

Likewise, Boyd and his men had plenty of cover behind the trees, close to the river. They tied their horses off, and nestled in behind logs and small stumps.

Now the hard part, waiting and wondering. And they wondered how long they would have to wait and what would happen when the waiting was over.

Flying Eagle was with Sullivan, tied to a small tree, a gag in his mouth.

Sullivan looked at him, and then he looked at Bailey.

"You kind'a keep an eye on him. If he tries anything, kill'im. If any of his friends get in here amongst us, kill both of them quick."

Flying Eagle was not happy with what he was hearing. He shook his head, to no avail.

Sullivan kept looking at the well-worn trail that led up into the hills and the mountains. It was obvious the raiders drove their cattle up that trail. So they would be bringing them down it. A good stampede would come in handy.

After almost two hours, a lone rider came down the trail. He stopped when he reached the level ground. He looked around.

He slowly rode his horse over toward Sullivan's position.

He was looking at the ground, looking for tracks of any kind. He stopped, and drank from his canteen. He then turned around and slowly headed for the river. He got near the river and stopped.

He had not seen any of them or anything that was out of order. He went back up the trail.

It would not be long now, Sullivan knew.

Five minutes later, another rider came down the trail. He stopped and looked around just like the first one.

Then he rode on past where the Rangers were back in the direction they came from. He was out of their sight for a few minutes. He was obviously looking for the Comanches and their horses.

Then he came back and headed up the trail into the foothills. He never even looked down at the ground. If he had, he would have seen the Rangers' tracks.

Sullivan and the others breathed a sigh of relief.

But their waiting was about to be over.

Chapter Thirty-two

Sullivan held his Winchester in his hands. He looked down at it, then looked back toward the mountain trail. He was ready. He hoped all the Boys were. They were. He knew it.

They heard the bellowing of the cattle as they were driven down the trail toward one of the corrals. The Rangers could not see them yet, but they knew they were coming.

That knowledge created that funny feeling in their stomachs, a little tension, a little sweat.

Both corrals were off toward where Boyd and his men were, on that side of the big open clearing. So they would have closer, better shots at the raiders.

No matter. They all would have clear shots when they were out in the open.

"Remember, don't fire till I do," Sullivan whispered loudly.

Any minute now. Any minute now. They'll be here any minute now.

Then they saw them, the first of the cattle coming down the trail, being push hurriedly along.

"Wait . . . . wait . . . . wait."

Now raiders were seen on both sides of the cattle as more and more of them came into sight.

Sullivan would be looking for Jack the beast Stalker. He was the one he wanted to see dead. Kill him and his men and the havoc they produce goes away. He quickly thought about how he looks, what he was told. Rides a black horse, big man, dark beard, dark skin, dark hair, black coat.

He's the one. I'll kill him dead.

Now the cattle were rushing toward the corrals. Raiders were out front some guiding them into one.

All the cattle were down off the trail in the clearing.

And all the raiders, it appeared, were with them, along side them, behind them.

They were stirring up dust. The cattle were moving, moving, moving, like a tide coming in.

Must be two, three hundred head, something like that.

The raiders were waving their arms at the cattle, some with their hats in their hands. They were calling out to the cattle, encouraging them.

"Ge'dup!"

"Yo now!"

"Yih yih!"

"Move along now!"

"Yo cow!"

The cattle were responding, moving quickly toward the corral.

Must be twenty, twenty-five raiders. Where is he? Sullivan was thinking.

Then he spotted a big man on a big black horse. Dark beard, waving a black hat. That had to be him. One hundred yards away.

He aimed at him. Squeezed the trigger.

Bang!

The man on the black horse slumped.

Bang!

Bang!

Bang!

The Rangers with Sullivan began firing, and also those with Boyd!

Bang!

Bang!

Bang!

Bang!

Bang!

A hail of bullets was flying at the raiders from both directions!

The raiders pulled out their pistols and began returning fire!

Pow!

Pow!

Pow!

Pow!

Raiders were falling off their horses!

Cattle were stampeding!

Some toward the river!

Some back where they came from!

Where was Jack Stalker?

Dust was being stirred up!

Horses without riders were running in every direction!

Sullivan saw Jack Stalker turning his horse! He was hit, badly it looked like, but he was rushing back up the trail!

The firing continued from both Rangers and raiders!

Bang!

Bang!

Pow!

Pow!

Bang!

Pow!

Most of the raiders were down on the ground now!

A few of them raced toward the river right past Boyd!

A few went back up the mountain trail!

Sullivan stood up and ran for his horse!

He heard a sound, a loud sound coming toward the clearing!

A stampede of a hundred horses!

Chapter Thirty-three

The horses came charging into the clearing with Comanches trying to turn them to the corrals!

Two were out front of the horses leading them!

Some were besides them!

Some were behind them!

Horses and cattle became mixed together!

Now the horses broke free!

Some ran toward the river!

Some ran up the trail to the foothills!

Some came running toward Sullivan and his men!

The Comanches saw what was happening and they began firing at both groups of Rangers!

Bang!

Bang!

Bang!

Bang!

Sullivan and his men and Boyd and his men fired back at them!

Bang!

Bang!

Bang!

Five Comanches fell from their horses!

The rest of them headed for the river and Mexico following some of the horses and some horses followed them!

Now the shooting had stopped. Sullivan stood up to look at what was a battleground. He saw dead raiders and Indians. A few horses and cows were milling around, lost and not knowing what to do.

"Come on! Let's go get Stalker!" Sullivan said to his men.

They jumped on their horses, leaving Flying Eagle tied up.

They charged up the trail, not knowing where their hideout was and how far they had to go.

As they rode as fast as they could, Sullivan wondered what they would find. Would it be a simple cabin, a large house, a fortress? How many men went with him? Would they be together or spread out? All in one place, a house, or some in a barn?

After almost thirty minutes, they stopped and dismounted.

"Much further than I thought. We better rest these horses," Sullivan said.

Just then, Boyd and his men pulled up with them. They dismounted as well.

"What ya think?" Boyd asked.

"We won't know what we got till we get there. We could be ridin' into anything. But I wounded Stalker."

"How many men with him up there?"

"I don't know. I couldn't tell. Enough to be trouble, I know that."

After ten minutes, they mounted up and rode on.

Soon they were high in the mountains. They kept a close eye on the trees, wondering if they would be shot by somebody they could not see.

Finally, they came to a place where they could look down at a valley. There was a log house, rough looking, but sturdy it seemed. The large barn was the same. There were several corrals and holding pens for cattle.

"Well, there it is, Boys. That's what we're up against," Sullivan said.

"Look at those corrals," Boyd said. "What do ya see?"

"Not much. Only two horses."

"Where'd the rest of'em go?"

"Away from here if they're smart."

Sullivan thought a moment before he spoke.

"Here's what we'll do. Spread out and go in slow. Be where you can get cover. Some of ya head for the barn. Others of ya go on around to the right there. Get behind that house. Boyd, you go with'em."

"What are you gonna do?"

"I'm gonna slowly ride right straight in. Cover me some of ya. We'll see if anybody is at home. Let's go."

The Rangers moved out slowly, taking their time, keeping their eyes open, being careful.

After several minutes, some of then reached the barn. They got off their horses, looked inside. Then they went to the windows and doors where they would have a clear view of the house.

The other group went around to the right, beyond one of the corrals. They reached the back of the house, tied their horses to posts and rails, and sought cover.

Sullivan walked his horse as slow as he would go straight at the front door. When he reached the house, he stopped, got off his horse, and tied him to a rail. He stepped up on the porch and walked to the door. Holding his Winchester in his left hand, he pulled out his pistol. The door was ajar, with a slight opening. He put his left foot on the door and pushed it open.

By the fireplace, on his left, he saw two men on the floor, one lying down and the other sitting up propped against the hearth.

Sullivan stepped on inside and walked over to the men.

"Who are you?" he asked the one sitting up.

"Pete de Luca."

"Who is that?"

"Jack Stalker."

"Is he alive?"

"He died after we got here."

"How bad you hurt?"

"I'm gut shot. One in the back too. Ain't got long, I know."

"Can I help ya?"

"Got any whiskey?"

"Nope."

"Ya can't help me then."

"I would if I cold."

"Yeah."

Sullivan stood there looking at the two men.

Boyd came in the back door and looked at the men on the floor.

"Just checkin' on ya," he said.

"That's Jack Stalker there. Dead. That's Pete de Luca. He's about to be."

Pete de Luca looked up at them, slightly smiled, and fell over on the floor.

When they went outside, all the men gathered around.

"He's in there dead, and one of his men. Some of ya get'em in the ground. Bailey, I put you charge of Flying Eagle. You and Ted Kite go back down there and set him free. Let him go. And find our mules. Hope they didn't go to Mexico. We'll be along."

Chapter Thirty-four

Days later, Sullivan and Boyd and Company M of the Texas Rangers pulled into El Paso.

They were dirty, tired, worn out, but they had a feeling of accomplishment because of what they had done. They had rid that part of west Texas of a scourge upon the land.

They were ready now for rest, sleep, good food, and some were ready for some good drinking. The others were just ready for some more sleep.

They first went to the livery stable to put up their horses and saddles and the one mule they had left.

When Bailey and Kite got to where Flying Eagle had been left tied to the tree, they discovered he was gone. He had been nice enough to leave the one mule and most of their supplies, what was left of them after he took what he wanted. The other mules were gone to Mexico. They could not imagine a Comanche brave riding a mule bareback across the river and into Mexico. But he had surely done that.

After seeing to their horses, the Rangers went to their hotel, put their weapons and gear in their rooms, took baths downstairs in the back part of the first floor where there was a room for bathing. Outside was a well for drawing water. Inside was a pot belly stove for heating it. There were four large bathtubs. It took a while for all of them to have their turn. As each man finished bathing and dressed, he went to the hotel dining room. It wasn't long until they were all there seated at the tables. They enjoyed a meal of steak, beans, tomatoes, peppers, onions, bread, and coffee.

When the meal was over, they went down the street to one of the saloons. Sullivan had requested that they go there together. As soon as they were seated, he asked a waitress to bring glasses and a bottle. Drinks were poured for each man. Then he stood up before them.

"Boys, I wanted us to come here together so I could toast you for what you have done. We got shut of a mean villain, the worst kind. He is done for now, and won't be causing no more trouble and human sufferin'. You are a great bunch of Texas Rangers. Here's to ya."

Sullivan lifted his glass, as they all did, and then he sat down.

William Boyd then stood up and spoke.

"I want us to drink a toast to Clem Young, who died too young. But he gave his life for Texas and for all of us."

They all drank down the whiskey, and Sullivan called for another bottle.

George Bailey stood up to make a toast.

"I want us to raise our glasses to honor our leader, Captain Toombs Sullivan."

"Hear! Hear!"

Slim Dunken stood up to offer a toast.

"Here's to our fearless second in command, Sergeant William Boyd."

"Hear! Hear!"

Ted Kite stood up to make a toast.

"Here's to the great state of Texas."

"Hear! Hear!"

Sullivan ordered another bottle.

Roger Maples stood up to offer a toast.

"Here's to the great and wonderful and forever will be, the Confederate States of America."

"Hear! Hear!"

Sullivan called for another bottle.

Ronald Wildman stood up and spoke.

"I want to offer a toast to my dear sweet mother who raised me right . . . . and was . . . . always opposed to drinkin' whiskey . . . . which is why one dark . . . . night . . . . she . . . . what did she do . . . . oh, yeah she shot my daddy dead cause of his . . . . drinkin'. She said he . . . . had the right, uh, last name . . . . because he really was a wild man . . . . but not fer long."

"Hear! Hear!"

Ronald Wildman sat down, and then he stood back up.

"And . . . . another thing . . . ."

"Sit down, wild man!" Timothy Davis called out.

"Hear! Hear!

Other toasts were made to Alabama, Georgia, Jefferson Davis, Robert E. Lee.

Sullivan called out to the waitress.

"Bring two bottles this time!"

"Hear! Hear!"

"Right here!" Ronald Wildman was able to mutter.

"Hear! Hear!"

More toasts were made until they could not think of anything else worthy of one.

Finally, Sullivan stood back up and spoke again.

"All right, that is probably enough for tonight. You Boys got a few days off unless something happens and we need to get back to work. So rest up. Enjoy the time off."

"Hear! Hear!"

Chapter Thirty-Five

The next morning, most of the Rangers slept in. But not Sullivan. That was something he could never do.

He ate breakfast in the dining room. When he finished his meal, he got the attention of the waitress. She walked slowly over to his table.

"What would it be, Mister Texas Ranger?"

"Could I have another cup of coffee, please?"

"Sure, anything for you," she replied, with a big smile.

Soon she was back with a coffee pot. She poured his cup nearly full.

"If there's anything else you want or need, just let me know."

"You bet."

When Sullivan finished his coffee, he went to the stables to check on his horse and the other's as well.

After that, he stopped by to speak to Marshall Ted Wheeler.

When he went in the office, Wheeler looked up and spoke.

"Morning, Sullivan. Have a seat."

"How are you, Marshall?"

Sullivan sat down across from Wheeler in front of his desk.

"I am well. I see you are back. How did you do?"

"Jack the beast Stalker is no more. We found him and his men down south in the Quitman Mountains. Oddly enough, he was about to swap a bunch of cattle for a bunch of horses the Comanches brought there in the middle of a battle with Stalker and his men. We killed a lot of both. The Comanches went to Mexico real quick. We followed Stalker up in the mountains to his hideout. A cabin. He was dead by the time we got to him, and one of his men. Where the rest of'em went I got no idea."

"That is excellent. That puts a stop to a lot of meanness around these parts."

"Yep. I'm glad about that."

"So what now for y'all?"

"We just wait for the next report about an Indian raid.

Too bad we can't be out there to stop'em before they happen."

"Yeah. You'd never know where to be ahead of time."

"What's happening here in town?"

"It's the usual, Sullivan. You know, a few drunks here and there, a man killed for being with another man's wife, I can't blame anybody for that, hang a horse thief now and then."

"Sounds like fun, the kind I had when I was a deputy in Fort Worth for a while, in between stints as a Ranger."

"Oh, how did that come about?"

"It's a long story, like most of'em, and not worth tellin'."

"Sure."

"What's happenin' out at the fort?"

"Not much I don't guess. Only contact I really have is when some soldier comes to town and gets drunk."

"Well, I'll move along, Marshall. You got work to do. Think I'll go out to the fort just to check in and let Colonel Kicklighter know about the success we had with Jack Stalker. Keep the peace, Marshall."

"Always something. Thanks for stopping in."

Sullivan left the Marshall's office and went to pick up his mail, if there was any, and he was hoping there would be.

He walked in the El Paso General Store where in one corner there was what served as the post office. The store owner, a Mister John G. Moore, was the official Post Master for the City of El Paso. He was a pudgy little man, mostly bald, and he wore wire-rimmed glasses.

"Welcome," Mister Moore said, as Sullivan walked in.

"Howdy. I'd like to see if I got any mail."

"Name, Sir?" Moore asked, as he walked over to the post office counter.

"Toombs Sullivan."

"Oh, you are the Texas Ranger."

"Yep. One of'em."

"Well, good. Let me see. I think you got something here if I can just find it. Here it is. Captain Toombs Sullivan, Texas Rangers, El Paso, Texas. Mailed from Austin, Texas. Well. Captain, eh. That sounds important."

"It ain't."

Sullivan held out his hand, reaching for the letter.

"Oh," said Moore. "Here ya go."

"Thanks."

Sullivan stepped outside and sat down on a wooden bench in front of the large window. He opened the letter and read it.

My Love,

I hope this letter finds you doing well. I think

of you constantly (Constance, get it?) and miss

you more than I could express in written

words. I am doing fine. My teaching is rewarding.

The children are progressing nicely. Not

any real news from here, other than I can

hardly wait to see you again. But I know

I must. Take care of yourself. I will do

the same.

Love with all my heart,

Constance

Sullivan held the letter up and smelled the perfume.

He stood up, placed the letter in the pocket of his coat, and walked down the street.

Chapter Thirty-six

For the next two weeks, Company M of the Texas Rangers stationed at El Paso, Texas, saw no real action in their role as protectors of the people of west Texas. They spent their time taking care of their equipment, gear, weapons, and horses, always ready at any moment to answer any call for help. But no request ever came in. It seemed that all was quiet in that part of the state.

On a Monday morning, Captain Toombs Sullivan had a note waiting for him at the hotel desk, when he came downstairs for breakfast. He unfolded it and read it on his way to a table in the dining room.

Captain Sullivan, please come out to the fort and see me. I have some information for you.

Colonel Anthony Kicklighter

U S Army

Fort Bliss, Texas

When Sullivan sat down, he looked at the note again, and wondered what that could be.

The waitress brought him a cup of coffee.

"What'll it be, Mister Texas Ranger?"

"The usual, please," he replied, without even looking up.

In a few minutes, she brought out his plate of three fried eggs, a small piece of steak, biscuits, and gravy.

Sullivan ate hurriedly, wondering what could be so important. He had another cup of coffee.

When he was finished with his meal, he left the hotel and went to the stable, saddled his horse, and headed for Fort Bliss.

Ten minutes later, he walked into Colonel Kicklighter's office. The colonel stood up when he saw Sullivan, and came around his desk to shake his hand.

"Have a seat, Captain."

"Thank you, Colonel."

"As my note indicated, I have some news for you."

"Good or bad?"

"It is not good. Ten, maybe twelve miles east of here, a rancher was wiped out. His cattle were stolen, house and barn burned down. He was killed. No females were found there, but it was obvious there was at least one there, a wife, I was told. It was not Comanches or Apache. No indication at all that any Indians were involved. No sign of them. Nothing there that shows it was them. No Indian style killing of the man, just shot once. But hear this. "There was a witness. A young Mexican, maybe fifteen, worked for them. He said it was white men. He said it was Jack the beast Stalker. He had known about him, had seen him a time or two.

"I told him Stalker was dead. He said that is not true. He is very much alive."

"That can't be true," Sullivan replied. "I shot him myself. I wounded him, and followed him to his cabin, just like I told you. I went in there and he was dead. My men buried him."

"How close were you when you shot him?"

"Maybe a hundred yards."

"Tell me what you shot at?"

"What ya mean? How he looked? Dark man, dark beard, wore black, black hat, black horse."

"Did he have a sign around his neck that said, my name is Jack?"

"What?"

"The description you gave could have been anybody. Maybe he was a decoy he sent out, an imposter, a look a like. Maybe he just stayed home that day."

"But I saw him dead."

"You saw dead the man you shot."

"Yeah."

Sullivan thought a minute. Kicklighter looked at him.

Sullivan's face turned red. He was more than agitated at this news he could hardly believe. But he knew. He knew it was true.

"All right. We'll go get him. Again. This time I'll make sure."

"It might not be easy. The Boy said he has a large army with him, his words. He has recruited a group of Mexican bandits to ride with him, according to our witness."

"That makes it interesting."

"I will be at your disposal. We are not now involved in any operation. So we will be available to help you with this. Now we cannot go out with you in your search for him and them. It could take more than days, maybe weeks, to locate him. When you find him, then you send a man to get us, and we will be there with you. He has to be stopped."

"All right, Colonel. I appreciate the help. We'll need it, if he has a larger group with him. We'll pull out as soon as we can ready ourselves. We'll be in touch."

Both men stood up and walked to the door of the outer office.

"Take care, Captain."

"Thank you, Sir."

Chapter Thirty-seven

That night, Sullivan gathered the Rangers around their dinner tables which were in the far right corner of the hotel dining room.

"Boys, I went out to see the colonel at the fort today. He requested that I see him. He had some news for us. There have been some raids on ranchers and farmers, just like there were before we killed Jack Stalker. Here's the worst part of what he said to me. These raids are by any even larger group of raiders

and they are being led by Jack Stalker."

"What?" exclaimed Timothy Davis.

"Yeah, it's true. He was seen by a witness at one of'em. The man we buried was not him. None of us ever saw him before. We just had a description. I shot a dark man with a dark beard and a dark hat on a black horse. Stalker was not even there at all. He sent that man as a look-alike, I guess. Anyway, we got to go after him again, and this time we gonna kill him for sure.

"Now, his group is bigger. Colonel Kicklighter said the army will help us. When we locate him and his men, we will send for the cavalry before we go in.

"I know you ain't happy about this. I ain't happy about this, but that is our job. It is what we do, like it or not.

"We have had a good rest now. The horses are rested and well fed. Our equipment is in good shape, weapons ready.

"Davis, you and Bailey find us three mules. Kite and Maples, get all our stuff together, ready to go. Wildman, go see the Marshall, see if he got a wanted poster with Stalker's mug on it. Should have had that before. We got to make sure this time.

"Any other thoughts by anyone?"

Sullivan looked around at the men. They looked at each other. Some of them shook their heads, meaning no.

"We head out day after tomorrow. Have a good night. Drinks at the saloon tonight, put of my tab, but don't over-do it."

With that, the Rangers left and went down to the saloon they liked best.

Willam Boyd stayed behind. He and Sullivan sat back down.

"What do ya think?" Sullivan asked.

"I don't know," Boyd replied. "Could be tough this time, tougher than before."

"I know. That worries me."

"At least we'll have the cavalry with us. That should be the deciding factor."

Sullivan thought a moment, before he replied.

"Yeah. But it depends on where we are don't it. And how long it takes for them to reach us. We could be in a real mess, if they discover us before we discover them. I can see us now."

"Like always, we got to look on the bright side," Boyd suggested. "The sun gonna come up every day, and it gonna shine down on us. It always has. We been in some rough spots before, but don't we always come out of them? Yes, of course we do. We got something good on our side. Call it providence, fate, whatever. We ain't gonna bite off more than we can chew. We'll be fine. Don't worry."

"I wish I was as sure about this as you are."

"Mark my word."

"I'm holdin' you to that."

"Well," Boyd said, as he stood up, "I'm gonna go join the Boys, have one myself, and make sure they don't have too many."

"Good. See ya in the mornin'."

Sullivan stayed at the table a while. Then he went up to his room.

He sat down on his bed for a moment. He got up and moved to the table that served as his official unofficial office. He pulled out a piece of paper and began writing.

Dear Constance,

I am writing to let you know I am doing good. We have

had a restful couple of weeks. The men are in good shape

and seem to be doing well.

No real news over this way. Just the routine kinds of

things going on here.

In a couple of days we are going out on patrol. This

is just the normal thing we do. Don't expect to run

into any trouble. We want to check with ranchers and

be sure they are all doing fine. We expect they will

be.

We could be gone a couple of weeks or even longer, so

don't expect a letter from me any time soon.

Take care of yourself.

Your loving husband,

Toombs

He sat there reading through his letter a few times. He then put it in an envelope, sealed it, and addressed it.

"What she don't know won't hurt her," he said out loud to himself and nobody.

Chapter Thirty-eight

As they were saddling their horses, getting ready to leave,

Sullivan looked over at Boyd and spoke to him.

"I don't know where to start on this, unless we go back to his cabin and see if he's there or still uses it or what."

"I think you're right. I been thinking the same thing. We got no clue other than to just do that."

"All right. We'll do it. Course, we could run up on some victim before we get there."

"Always possible."

Fifteen minutes later, Sullivan led the Rangers up the street headed south-east toward where they had first fought the raiders. They followed the river along.

Despite all he could do, he could not get rid of the uneasy feeling he had.

He turned around in his saddle and looked back.

"Davis, take the point!"

"Got it!" Davis replied, as he rode by Sullivan and Boyd.

Davis soon disappeared.

By mid-afternoon, they had made good time and were far down along the river.

Off to the east, they saw smoke along the horizon.

"That can't be but one thing," Boyd said, as suddenly they all stopped.

"You're right," Sullivan answered. "Wonder if Davis has seen it and gone that way."

"Want me to go check it out and see if he's over there?"

"Sure. Go take a look. We'll move slowly along this way and wait on ya before we come there."

"I'll let you known soon."

"Good."

Boyd rode off to the east toward the smoke they had seen.

Sullivan and the other Rangers sat there for a few minutes.

"If that is Stalker," he said to them, "then we have found him a lot sooner than I thought."

"Maybe it's Comanches," George Bailey suggested.

"Could very well be."

There minutes later, they began hearing shots fired there in the distance.

"Let's go!" Sullivan shouted to the men.

Off they went as quickly as they could, following the way Boyd had gone.

Soon they were over a hill looking down at a burning house and barn.

There was a man kneeling by a wagon firing at Comanches!

Bang!

Bang!

Bang!

A woman and a child were kneeling beside him!

The Comanches were circling the house!

Boyd and Davis were still on their horses chasing the Comanches!

They were firing their pistols!

Pow!

Pow!

Pow!

Two Comanches fell from their ponies!

Sullivan and the Rangers raced to join the fight!

Soon they were in the middle of it!

They were firing their pistols now!

Pow!

Pow!

Pow!

Pow!

Two more Comanches fell to the ground!

What looked like their leader suddenly yelled out something!

They all turned and began heading south away from the ranch!

When the Rangers reached the house, they joined the man and woman as they began drawing water from the well and trying to put out the fire!

Most of the house was made of large stones, so it was not burning. Only part of the roof was on fire.

They quickly put it out.

The same was true of the barn. They turned to it next. Soon that fire was out. Much of the smoke had come from stacks of hay near the barn, an old wagon, and stacks of lumber and firewood. Soon they had saved most of the barn.

When all the fires were out, they talked with the man and woman.

The young man was tall and rawboned. He had distinct facial features, large jaws, strong chin, brown hair, black looking eyes. The young woman was small, blond, blue eyes, fine facial features, a wonderful smile. Their daughter was about five or six years old it appeared. She was tiny and blond like her mother.

"We're Texas Rangers," Sullivan said to the couple.

"Show glad you come along. Just in time. I'm Johnny Stalworth. Wife, Emmie. Girl's Emmalou."

"I'm glad we did too."

Stalworth stuck out his hand to Sullivan and then Boyd.

"Name's Toombs Sullivan."

"I'm William Boyd. That there is Timothy Davis."

"Proud to meet you fellers."

"Me too," said Emmie.

"This ever happen before?" Sullivan asked.

"Why you think this house is made of stone? About three year ago they burnt down the first house we had here. Nothing left standing but the chimney. When I saw that chimney standing solid and proud, I said to myself, well why not. Hence a stone house. Been trying to figure out how to have a fireproof roof, but not been able to do it yet. Same with the barn. I think it makes them mad when they see a stone house."

"I bet it does. Say, you mind if we camp here tonight on yore property?"

"Be glad to have you all. Sure."

"I'll fix your supper. We got plenty," Emmie said.

"Oh, don't go to no trouble count of us," Sullivan replied.

"No trouble," she answered. "You not only saved us a lot of trouble. You saved our lives and our house."

"Well, fine then. Say, Johnny. I see ya got a lot of lumber and stuff they didn't have time to burn up. What if we help you make yore repairs tomorrow. Won't take long if all of us are at it."

"That is most generous," Stalworth replied. "I appreciate it very much and accept your offer."

When he got a chance, Boyd spoke to Sullivan.

"You wanna send for Kicklighter and the cavalry?"

"Nope. We ain't got time to wait on them. We'll do the killin' ourselves."

Chapter Thirty-nine

The Rangers made their camp for the night out away from the house.

Except for damage to about half of the roof, the house would be habitable. The roof over the kitchen and the main bedroom was fine.

Emmie Stalworth began preparing the evening meal, as the Rangers set up their camp about fifty yards away from the house.

Later Sullivan, Boyd, and Davis joined them at the kitchen

table which was large enough for only six people. The other Rangers ate outside sitting around on whatever they could find.

Emmie served them a fine meal of steak, fried potatoes, green beans, onions, and cornbread. And she prepared the best coffee they had ever had. She boiled the coffee with milk and sugar already in it. It was the first down-home kind of meal any of them had eaten in a long time.

"Tell me about yourselves," Sullivan said, as they began eating.

"What's there to tell? We came out here like so many other people chasing a dream. We both grew up just north of Memphis. We both grew up on farms, I mean large ones. We had slaves like so many other people, but we did not live on plantations. None of that stuff. We treated them well. They were like family members to us. I fought in the war. When I got home, there weren't nothin' left to speak of. Our church was still there and so was the preacher, so we got married, loaded up that wagon that was right out there until today, now it ain't, and came out here. It weren't no big decision, should we, should we not. We had no choice. Both my folks was in the ground. Died of natural causes I guess. Cause they did. You talk," Johnny said, looking over at Emmie.

"Well, my situation was just like his, except I was there to watch it. My folks made me hide in the barn when the Yankees came. They killed my Pa because he stood up to them when they were going to take our milk cow and some chickens. Shot him dead in front of our house, in front of Ma. Me and her was unharmed. They went on off. We had to bury Pa all on our own. Not any men folk around to dig a grave. We dug it. Within a year Ma died of a broken heart. I went down the road to live with my aunt and a cousin. Life was hard, but we lived through it. When Johnny came home, it was not a hard decision to make, coming to Texas."

"Yeah," Johnny said. "We come all the way over here on this side of the state to get away from all the people who were coming to Texas. We was all alone for a good while. Nobody bothered us, except for the Indians, now twice. But now we got close neighbors, too close. One of'em that way about five mile, and the other about eight, ten mile that way. They found us."

"You have any concern about a continuing Indian threat," Sullivan asked.

"Of course I do now. This is their second try. They would have gotten us, but you Boys ran them off. What's gonna happen next time? I don't know."

There was silence for a moment because Sullivan, Boyd, and Davis knew what would happen next time. Sullivan knew he had to fill the air with some kind of statement that did not scare them to death right there.

"Well," he said, "likely they were just a band out huntin' and came upon you. They probably with a large tribe that has moved on down south. Just be prepared. Dig you a hiding place under this house. Tunnel out some way from it so if they ever burn it down, it won't fall in on you. If they burn it down, they will think you did not live through that and will not dig through the ashes and boards to find ya. Fight'em off as best you can, then hide in the tunnel."

"Sounds like good advice," Johnny said.

Later on, as Sullivan and Boyd were bedding down, Boyd had a question.

"Do you really think they can survive another attack?"

"No. Not a chance. They're lucky we came along. Next time, won't be nobody around. Them far-off neighbors might see the smoke, but they can't get here to help. Too late. The tunnel just might work. Might not. He might not dig it."

The next morning, the repair work began. There was plenty of wood still left to re-roof the portions of the house and barn that needed it. One team worked on the house. Another team worked on the barn. Two more Rangers went to the wood pile and made shingles for both roofs.

Then that next day, the Rangers prepared their horses and mules for the journey. When they were saddled up and loaded up, they went to tell the Stalworths goodbye.

"We wish you well," Sullivan said, hoping it would be that way, fearing it would not.

"Thanks so much for saving our house and barn, and most of all for saving our lives," Johnny said.

"We'll never forget you," Emmie added.

"Sure," Sullivan said. "We'll be on our way now."

"Be careful," Emmie said.

Sullivan smiled at her, nodded his head, and mounted his horse.

Chapter Forty

Shortly before noon, Timothy Davis came riding back to the column of Rangers. He stopped, when he reached Sullivan and Boyd.

"We got a man and his family coming up behind me. He's got a story you need to hear."

They waited on the wagon to reach them. When it had, the man stopped it.

It was a man and women in the wagon. Two teenage boys were

behind them on two horses. Two mules were pulling the wagon which was loaded down with what looked like everything they owned.

The man appeared to be in his fifties. He was unshaven and rough looking. He wore an old black coat that looked like it had once been part of a suit. He had a wide black hat on his head. It too had seen its better days. The woman wore a blue dress with little red dots and an old hat on her head. She appeared to be the same age as her husband, and it seemed she had lived a hard life. The two boys were wearing brown pants and faded blue shirts. They also had on old hats.

"You folk Texas Rangers, eh?"

"That's right. How can we help ya?" Sullivan asked.

"Ya can't help me now, other than gettin' out of my way.

Ya could have yesterday or sooner, I reckon."

"What happened?"

"My cattle got stole. Ain't the first time neither. But they cleaned me out this time."

"Who did it? Where's yore place? What happened?"

"You shore ask a lot of questions all in a row. I didn't see who it was, but I think I know. Before and this time too, it's a big group of white men. Cattle thieves. Might be a few Mexs mixed in with'em. I know who it is. It's that man they call the beast. Seen him good that first time. This time they got everyone of them. What with them and fightin' off Indians from time to time, I done had enough."

"So they didn't burn you out?"

"Nope. Neither time."

"Don't sound like him, Jack Stalker. The beast."

"Oh, it's him all right."

"He usually kills people and burns down everything, just like Comanches."

"He spares us. Except for the cattle. Least he left our horses and mules so we could leave."

"How you know it was him?"

"Cause by hisself he came upon my Boys fishing down at the creek one day. He got off his horse and talked to them. They fixed him up a pole and he sat down by them. They caught some fish. They cooked them right there cause he said he was hungry.

He seemed like a nice man, they said. He asked their names and where they lived. They said we are Jack and Joe Thomas, and we live over the next two hills. He said his name was Jack Stalker. I'm George Thomas, and this is Katie. He wanted to know if all these cows out there were theirs. They said, yes, Pa's. Yore Pa know how many he got? He wanted to know. They said yeah, a little over two hundred. The next day about a hundred were gone.

That was about two year ago. He came back day fore yesterday and got the rest. He didn't kill us neither time 'cause he liked the Boys, I'm guessin'."

"I'm sorry this happened to you."

"Me too."

"Where you goin'?"

"Back to Arkansas. Never should have left. Got the Texas fever, I guess."

"And yore place is where?"

"Ain't mine no more. Got shut of it. Bout twelve, fifteen mile back that way. Can't miss it. You can have it."

"We wish you all well and a safe journey."

"You too. We'll be off now. Got a long road to travel. Get up!" he said, as he snapped the reins on the backs of the mules.

The Rangers watched them as they moved on and waved at the two Boys. The Boys smiled and waved back.

"That's what we are out here to prevent," Sullivan said. "But we didn't do them no good."

"What now?" Boyd asked.

"Let's go take a look at their place."

The Rangers rode south and reached the Thomas ranch late in the afternoon. They sat on their horses and looked around. It seemed like the perfect set-up. There was a nice looking house, a large barn, ample corral area, a well close to the house.

"Looks like they got everything they need here," Boyd said.

"Yep," Sullivan replied. "Everything except what they came here for. Cattle to raise and sell."

"They got what we need for tonight."

"What is that, William?"

"A place to cook and sleep inside."

"You talked me into it. Take care of yore horses, Boys!"

Chapter Forty-one

The men put their horses and mules in the corral, after letting them drink water from the two troughs. There was plenty of hay around to feed them. Their saddles and gear were placed in the barn.

"Boys," Sullivan called out, "those of you who can cook, get at it. The rest of ya find them some firewood and then check out the house. See if they left anything we can eat tonight and anything we can take with us."

Those who would cook went inside. The others started

gathering up some firewood and taking it in the house.

After looking around some, Sullivan walked inside. He was met by Boyd.

"You need to see what those poor people left here," Boyd said.

"Show me."

"Right this way."

They walked through the kitchen to a storage room just off the back porch. They stepped inside.

"Look at this," Boyd said. "All these canned veggies and fruit. There's a potato bin stuffed almost full. Look up there, two hams."

"My goodness," Sullivan responded. "We're not only set for tonight, but for this trip as well."

"Also, I'll show you this. Follow me."

They walked back through the kitchen to the middle of the house.

"Three bedrooms with a double bed in one. One room has two cots, and the third has a double bed and a cot. That means seven of us can sleep in beds tonight."

"I'll sleep in the big living room on the floor," Sullivan said. "Since I don't sleep very well anyway, I may as well take up space on the floor, rather than staying awake in a bed somebody could use."

"Yeah, I'll take the floor too. Let the Boys get the best rest."

Later that evening, The Rangers sat at one long table in the kitchen. There was plenty of fried ham on a large platter. There were bowls of beans, squash, okra, fried potatoes, stewed apples, and another platter of pieces of cornbread. One of the men made coffee the way they had just had it with milk and sugar boiled in it. They found a big jug of milk at the end of a rope in the well.

"Sullivan," said George Bailey, "why can't we just stay here and let Indians and raiders come to us? Be a lot easier on us and the animals too."

"That ain't a bad idea, but it ain't what the State of Texas is paying us to do. They paying us to go get'em."

"Well, that settles it then," Bailey said, with a wide grin.

When the men finished their meal, they began cleaning up the kitchen and washing everything they had used.

"Hey," Sullivan said, "some of you cooks take a look out there in that storge room. See what we can take with us. We need as much of that stuff as we can handle. We'll put it to good use."

Later that evening, the Rangers began settling in. They picked out which bed they wanted. Some went outside and sat and stood around smoking.

Sullivan and Boyd went to check on the horses, making sure they were secure for the night.

When the two of them laid their bedrolls by the fireplace,

Boyd asked Sullivan a question.

"What are ya thinking about tomorrow?"

"They got a what, three, four day lead on us. I guess we pick up their trail and hope they stop for an extended rest along the way. I want out of here early in the morning and we'll ride late into the evening. Maybe we can gain a little ground on them. That man had no doubt it was Stalker and his raiders cause they weren't scalped or killed or damaged in any way because of the Boys knowing him."

It wasn't long until Boyd was asleep.

Sullivan lay awake on his back, looking at the ceiling. He was wondering what the next few days might bring. Another confrontation with the raiders was waiting, and this time they might not be so lucky.

A couple of hours passed by. He heard the horses making noises. Something was upsetting them he thought. He picked up his pistol and went to the door. He quietly opened it slowly and peeped outside. They were prancing around some, unhappy about something. He could not see anything or anyone.

He slipped out the door and stood for a moment in the shadows. His eyes adjusted to the darkness.

There was only one thing to do.

Chapter Forty-two

Sullivan hesitated for a moment. He had to walk out toward the corral, but he did not want to do it. There was somebody or something out there.

He cocked his pistol and held it up waist high. He slowly walked across the yard toward the corral. When he reached it, he stopped to look around.

He heard something behind him, someone coming up on him, walking quickly behind him.

He turned around and saw Boyd coming to him.

"What is it?" Boyd whispered.

"I don't know. Something upset the horses. The mules don't care."

"Can't see nothin'"

"I'm goin' through the corral to the other side. You go around the other side of the barn. Don't shoot each other when we meet around there. And don't go in that barn by yoself."

Boyd walked to their left and went toward the other side of the barn. When he reached the front door of the barn, he stopped to listen. He heard nothing.

He then looked inside, while trying not to be seen. He could not see anything. He hurried across the front of the open doorway. He looked around the corner of the building, and saw no one. Then he slowly walked along the side of the building, moving carefully, cautiously.

When he reached the other end of the barn, he stopped and listened. He heard nothing.

Sullivan crawled though the fence. He stood in the middle of the animals. They seemed to calm down some with him next to them, as though they knew he was there to protect them.

He walked slowly toward the other side. When he reached it, he slid through the fence and stood there for a moment. He heard nothing and saw nothing.

He eased his way toward the barn. When he reached it, he stood by the door, waiting for Boyd.

In a moment, Boyd was standing on the other side of the door. They could see each other.

They stepped inside and began moving toward the front of the barn. They took it a step at a time, each of them expecting someone to jump out on them. Soon they reached the front door.

They stood outside for a moment, looking and listening. There was no one there.

"It wasn't just me," Sullivan said. "Something or somebody upset the animals."

"Whoever it was, he's gone now, or maybe just hiding where we can't see him."

"If he or they were in the barn, they could've jumped us real easy."

They walked back over to the house, with Sullivan still wondering who it was. He knew somebody had been there. When they reached it, Boyd went inside first. Sullivan stood in the doorway looking back at the barn and corral and listening. Then he went inside and closed the door.

Boyd laid back down and was back to sleep in no time.

Sullivan lay on his bedroll, wide awake and would be for a long time. From experience, he knew the Comanches were always with them, always wanting their horses. They were willing to face any kind of danger to get them.

He had not placed any guards outside that night. He knew now that was a mistake. He just thought they were nowhere near any Indians, and being in the house everything would be fine.

Now he knew he was wrong, and he knew what he should have done.

The next morning, the Rangers were up before dawn, wanting to get an early start. But before leaving a hearty breakfast was in order.

Those who did the cooking prepared a meal of flapjacks, molasses, butter, fried ham, and strong coffee.

When the meal was finished, they loaded up all the food they could take with them, the hams, canned goods, flower, sugar, coffee. They packed it all on the mules.

They got their horses saddled and waited for the sun to creep up over the eastern horizon so they would be able to see any tracks they would need to follow.

While they were waiting, Boyd disappeared for a few minutes.

The dark skies turned gray, then lightened up, then the sun was just above the eastern hills. They could see now.

Suddenly Boyd was back. He walked over to Sullivan who was standing by his horse.

"Found'em," Boyd said.

"What would that be?" Sullivan asked, with a half smile.

"Footprints. Not no boots either."

"Comanch?"

"Sure as Grandma wore bloomers."

"All right, saddle up!"

Chapter Forty-three

"Davis!" Sullivan called out, as they began to leave the ranch.

"Got it!" Davis replied, knowing that Sullivan meant for him to take the point.

Davis rode past Sullivan and Boyd, hurrying off ahead of the column.

It was not long until he came back to them.

"I found the tracks where they took that heard of cattle

away to the south."

"Take us there," Sullivan replied.

The company followed Davis for about two miles. Then he stopped, and they did as well.

Davis, Sullivan, and Boyd dismounted. They walked around looking at the ground.

"Shod horses," Boyd said.

"That'd be them," Sullivan said. "Go on now and see where they take us."

"Right," Davis replied, as they mounted back up and he rode away.

The Rangers followed Davis and the tracks all day.

They stopped several times to rest the horses and the mules.

They also stopped at noon for a light lunch of beef jerky and water. Then they resumed their journey.

Late in the afternoon, they came to a creek. The water was cool and clear and crisp looking.

"This would be a good place to stop for the night," Sullivan said. "You know what to do. Have at it."

The Rangers let their horses and mules drink water in the creek. Then they ran a line from one tree to another, took the saddles off the horses, and tied the reins to the line.

While some unloaded the mules, others gathered wood for three fires.

Three tables were set up. A large ham was set down on one of them. Frying pans were place over the fires, along with pots, and two coffee pots were prepared.

It was not long until the men were eating a meal of fried ham, beans, potatoes, and coffee.

When the meal was over, they washed the pots and pans and utensils in the creek.

They spread out their bedrolls near the fires.

Then Boyd posted the guards and gave them the schedule.

"Bailey and Dunken, first watch. Then Kite and Maples, Easom and Wildman, me and Canton."

As the sun began to hang low over the west, Bailey and Dunken took their watches at each of the camp, along the creek.

Boyd saw Sullivan standing on the eastern side of their camp, looking down toward the south.

"Ain't like him to not be back here by supper time," Boyd said.

"Just what I was thinking," Sullivan answered.

"Reckon sompin' got him?"

"I sure hope not. Maybe he got lost."

"Want me to go look for him?" Boyd asked.

"Nope. Ya couldn't find him in the dark. Can't lose two of ya. He'll get back here. Or maybe he won't. We'll know by in the mornin'."

The Rangers were up as soon as the sun chased away the darkness and began lighting up the sky. Soon rays of the sun were shining down into the camp.

When Boyd saw Sullivan, he walked over to him.

"He never came back," Boyd said.

"Yeah. I know."

"Think we'll find him?"

"He won't be finding us."

As soon as the men could heat the fires back up, boil the coffee, and eat ham left over from the night before, they loaded everything back onto the mules. Soon they were saddled up and ready to ride.

Sullivan looked around at the men. Before he could say anything, Boyd spoke.

"I'll take the point," he said, as he rode off.

"I guess all of ya know Davis did not come home last night.

Keep your eyes open for anything and everything. Maybe we'll find'im."

With that, Sullivan waved his right hand forward and they were off and following Boyd.

Boyd was following the trail of the cattle herd. It was plain to see where it went.

Two hours later, he went over a little rise and saw something there in the distance that made him stop. He got off his horse and tied its reins to a small tree. He pulled out his pistol and slowly approached. He drew near cautiously. He looked all around, making sure he was not about to be ambushed.

He did not know if he should go back and get the others or just wait on them. They could not be far behind him.

Chapter Forty-four

Boyd was still standing in the same spot when Sullivan and the company caught up with him. They came over the rise and saw him in the middle of the trail of cattle tracks. In the distance, they could see he was looking up at something.

When they reached him, they all dismounted and joined him, all of them looking up at the same thing he was staring at.

Timothy Davis was hanging by his neck. He looked like he had been beaten badly. His face was bruised and bloody. His hands

were tied behind his back. His gun belt and boots were missing.

Around his neck was not only the rope, but also a sign written on a large piece of paper. The message was written in large letters.

THIS MAN IS A CATTLE THEIF

HE TIRED TO TAK

OR COWS BUT WE STEPPED HYM

The Rangers were speechless for a few minutes. They just stood here looking at Davis.

"All right, cut him down." Sullivan said slowly. "Get the shovels."

Timothy Davis was lowered down to the ground. While two of the men were digging the grave near the tree and in the shade of its limbs, several others were cleaning Davis up some, doing the best they could to wash the dried blood from his face.

They laid him out on a blanket, and folded his arms over his chest. They combed his hair. Then the blanket was folded over him.

Four of the Rangers picked him up, took him to the grave, suspended him with two ropes, and then lowered him into the ground.

The men stood around the grave, looking down at Timothy Davis.

After several minutes of silence, Sullivan spoke.

"Well men, we have lost a friend and a good Ranger now. I wish I could tell his Mama, if he has one, what a fine young man he was. He died bravely in the line of duty for the state of Texas, and for us as well. He took what could'a been done to any of us. Guess he took it instead of one of us who'da been out here instead of him. So we send him now back to where he came from, to his father and his father's people, and may he be gathered unto them.

"Sergeant Boyd read the Bible and pray."

William Boyd read the Twenty-third Psalm and said the prayer.

Then Sullivan spoke to the Rangers again.

"Now we ain't chasing cattle and bad men no longer 'cause they broke the law. Now it's something personal. Now they started somethin' we gonna end. We gonna do to them and worse what they done to our man. Vengeance is mine saith the Lord. And it is gonna be our'ern as well. Let's ride."

"I'm gone!" Boyd shouted at Sullivan, as he rode out ahead of them.

Sullivan and the rest of the company then followed Boyd along the trail of the cattle tracks.

Three hours later, they caught up with Boyd. He was sitting on a small fallen tree waiting for them.

The Rangers dismounted and Boyd stood up to greet them.

"They spent the night right here. Then they headed off to the west there."

"Gone to Mexico," Sullivan said.

"Yep. Long gone now."

"Well, let's just go take a look at where they crossed," Sullivan suggested.

"Fine by me," Boyd replied.

The Rangers got back on their horses and headed off to the west, toward the river.

Soon they were letting their horses drink the waters of the Rio Grande. The men drank it as well. Some went down stream a ways and relieved themselves.

"They're over there," Boyd said, matter of factly.

"Yep, there's the tracks going into the river, and they come out on the other side," Sullivan remarked.

"So what we gonna do?" Boyd asked. "We can't go get'em."

"Nope, and we don't need to. Know why? Cause they comin' back. They ain't gone to Mexico but for a little while. They'll make their deal, and they'll be back. And we'll be right here waitin' on'em, William. Waitin' on'em."

"Sounds like a good plan."

"A killin' plan."

Sullivan spit in the river, and then spoke to the men.

"Gather round here, Boys. Here's what we gonna do. They went on over to the other side as you can see. But they ain't gone forever. They comin' back. And when they come back, we'll be waitin' right here. And when they get here, back on this side we gonna kill'em all. All of'em, ya hear me. We gonna get some justice for Timothy Davis.

"So take the horses back yonder a way. Hide'em out, secure'em. Then come back here and find yoreselves good cover for when they arrive. Be safe for our welcome home party."

Chapter Forty-five

The Texas Rangers of Company M waited along the river.

Their horses and mules were tied off a hundred yards back behind them. They took what cover they could find, but it was not much. They hid behind large stones, fallen trees, in small gulleys, anywhere they could find protection. Half of them were to the right of the trail, and half were to the left.

"Now, wait till they get over on this side of the river in Texas. Don't shoot'em in Mexico. I'll fire the first shot,"

Sullivan instructed them.

And he was anxious to fire that first shot and many others behind it. Nobody wanted sweet revenge more than he did. He could almost taste sweet revenge.

There was little shade. The sun was hot that day. It beat down upon them and beat them down. They drank what water they

had, and when it was gone, they had no more. Sullivan told them they could not take a chance by going to the bank of the river to fill their canteens. They would just have to wait.

The hours slid by slowly, but they fully expected the raiders to come back that day.

The hours continued to wear on down. At five o'clock, the sun began to slowly pass on toward the west.

Sullivan was on the right side of the trail. He looked around at his men. He could tell they were out of water and very thirsty. He started to tell them to go to the river, figuring the raiders were not coming that day.

With a questioning expression, he looked over at Boyd on the other side of the trail. Boyd lifted up his shoulders and held up his open right hand, as if to say, I don't know or who knows.

Then Boyd looked across the river and pointed toward it.

"Here they come," he said quietly, with his left hand partially shielding his mouth.

Sullivan turned toward the river. They could see dust in the air, obviously stirred up by a large number of horses.

"Get ready, Boys," he said. "They're about to be amongst us."

The cloud of dust was getting larger and closer.

Then they saw the lead riders.

"Wait. Wait," Sullivan said.

The horses were splashing through the water!

The lead riders were in Texas now!

On they came, now stirring up Texas dust!

More splashing, as all of them crossed the river!

All of the raiders were now in Texas!

They were now almost even with Sullivan!

He held his Winchester to his shoulder!

Bang!

All the Rangers began firing at the raiders!

Bang!

Bang!

Bang!

Bang!

Raiders and horses began falling to the ground!

The horses struggled to get up!

They began running off in all directions!

Some of them were running back to the river and across it to Mexico!

Some of the raiders began getting back up, only wounded!

Some of them would never get up again!

Those who could, pulled out their pistols!

Pow!

Pow!

Pow!

"Cut'em down!" Sullivan shouted!

The Rangers cut them down!

Then some of the raiders threw down their pistols!

They quickly held their hands in the air!

"We surrender!" some of them shouted!

"Hold yore fire!" Sullivan yelled.

The Rangers stopped shooting and they all stood up, coming out from behind their cover.

The Rangers walked toward the raiders. So this is what they look like, some of the Rangers thought.

"Keep yore hands in the air!" Sullivan yelled at them. "Move a finger and you'll be dead!"

None of the raiders moved a finger.

There were eleven raiders standing. Close to twenty were on the ground dead.

"Boyd, see if you can find Stalker."

"Got it," Boyd replied, as he turned back from those still alive and began looking at all the dead ones on the ground.

He walked among them, looking at each face. He rolled some of them over, so he could see them better.

Soon he was finished inspecting them.

"We ain't got no Stalker here," he reported.

"Where is he?" Sullivan asked the group of raiders.

"Who?" one of them replied.

"You know who!"

"I don't know who you talking about."

"Sure you do. Your boss, Jack Stalker."

"Never heard the name."

"What about you?" Sullivan said to another man.

"Don't know him."

"Y'all may be stupid, but we ain't. We know who you are, and we know who yore boss is."

"We ain't got no boss," another man said.

"Who did ya steal those cattle for?"

"What cattle?" the first man to speak asked.

"The ones you took to Mexico."

"We didn't take no cattle to Mexico."

"How did all these tracks get here?"

"Ain't got no idea."

"We been following you all the way here."

"Must have been somebody else."

"Fine. You didn't do it. Fine. But you gonna take the blame for it, and we'll do to you what we would'a done to them."

Sullivan turned to Boyd and nodded his head.

"Get'em ready, William."

Chapter Forty-six

"Take yore clothes off, all of'em!" Sullivan shouted at the raiders.

Slowly the raiders began undressing.

"What's the meaning of this?" one of the raiders asked.

"You'll find real soon."

"But we ain't done nothing."

"Well, you gettin' blamed for what was done and you gettin' the penalty."

"But we're innocent!" one of them screamed.

Sullivan walked over to him and stood in front of him.

He was young, not over nineteen or twenty Sullivan thought.

He was just a kid.

"I didn't do nothin'" he said.

"Oh, yeah. You did somethin'. You joined up with this gang of killers. That was yore big mistake. These men are yore friends. You gonna die with yore friends."

"Can you get word to my Mama? Tell her I didn't mean no harm. Tell her I just made a mistake and I am sorry. Sorry I disappointed her."

"I don't know yore Mama and don't care about yore Mama or you. If ya care about yore Mama, well then, you should'a listened to her to start with."

Sullivan turned around toward his men.

"Bailey, you and some of the boys find their horses. Well, any horses. Let's see," he said, turning back to look at the raiders, "get eleven horses."

"We going for a ride? Naked?" a raider asked.

"Oh yeah, you goin' for a ride all right."

Eleven horses were rounded up and brought to Sullivan.

He turned back to the raiders.

"Stealin' cows from other people is bad enough. It's against the law of the state of Texas. We are Texas Rangers, in case you didn't know. Our job is to enforce the laws of the state of Texas.

"But you did somethin' worse than stealin' other people's cows. You killed one of our men. You didn't kill him in a battle or a shootout or defendin' yoreself. You murdered him. You beat him to a pulp. Then you hanged him. He was a friend of ours. That hurt our feelin's real bad.

"So we can't let that pass. We gonna do to you what you done to him. But one thing extra. You naked now. Everythin' you are and everythin' you got is exposed to the world and all the animals and the birds.

"While you're hangin' from them trees over there, yore rotten butts gonna be eat away. They won't be nothin' left but bones hangin' from them trees.

"Any last words you wanna say?"

"I want to say I'm sorry," the youngest one said.

"Good. But too late. Anybody eles?"

"You ain't gonna really hang us are you?"

"Sure as night follows after day. Anybody else?"

"Shoot us dead instead of hanging us," one of them requested.

"Too quick and too easy. An easy way to die. We want it to last a little bit and have you dread it some. I'm hopin' it don't break yore necks, but instead ya just hang there a bit, chokin'."

"My god, man, this is insane," another raider said.

"Yep, God is the one ya best be callin' on, but it's a little late."

The Rangers led the horses over to a grove of trees a couple of hundred yards back away from the river. They were large trees, white oaks.

"Don't put more than one man to a limb," Sulivan said. "We don't want any limbs to break so they fall to the ground. Might hurt their little bare feet."

The horses were spread out among the trees. Ropes were placed around the necks of the raiders. They were made tight around them.

"Please don't do this!"

"Give us another chance"!

"Have some mercy on us!"

"Why don't you cry babies just shut up. You know we are guilty. We gettin' what's been coming to us. It all finally caught up with us. Be a man."

"Anything else anybody wants to say?" Sullivan asked.

Two of the raiders began crying, one of them was the youngest one.

"Help me, Jesus," another said.

Sullivan walked around behind the horses. He slowly pulled out his pistol. He looked at the backs of all eleven men.

Pow!

Pow!

"Get!"

The horses charged forward!

Eleven men were swinging back and forth.

Chapter Forty-seven

"We gonna just leave'em hangin' there?" asked Boyd.

"Yes, we are," answered Sullivan. "I made them a promise, and we gonna keep it. Get the Boys to round up them horses. We might need them, and I don't want Comanches gettin'em."

"All right, go get them horses!" Boyd called out.

As he walked away, Sullivan looked up at the eleven hanging men, still swaying just a little. He had administered justice in the best possible way, considering where they were.

It was a hard kind of justice, but they were in a hard country. They did not have time for niceties. They could not take them back to El Paso just to get the same result there. They would have hung in El Paso. It just would have taken a few days longer. That made no sense to Sulivan. They had to go after Jack the beast Stalker while there was still time to find him.

Minutes later, the Rangers came back to Sullivan having rounded up the horses.

"Make two strings of'em, five on one, six on the other. Bailey, you take one, Kite the other. Y'all can swap out later on down the road."

When the horses were roped together, Sullivan looked at them, and then mounted his own horse.

"Let's go."

As he said that, Boyd went on out ahead of them.

They made good time the rest of that day. In the late evening, they stopped to camp along the river. They went through their same routine, watering the animals, stringing them together between two trees, making the fires, unloading their supplies from the mules, cooking supper.

When the meal was ready, they sat around eating it. They felt lucky since none of them had been injured in the battle, such as it was. It was not much of a battle at all. It was instead an ambush. But that is what they needed to do.

They knew however, they had one more big battle coming up.

If Jack Stalker was indeed at his hide-out, he just might be hard to get out of there. They had no idea how many men he had with him or how they would be situated. But at the same time, they had again the element of surprise. Stalker had no idea about the events of that day. As far as he knew, his men were coming back with a good bit of money they had gotten from the cattle they had sold in Mexico. What he did not know would not hurt the Rangers.

When they were about finished eating, Boyd stood up.

"Wildman and Maples, take the first watch," he said.

"Sure, Boss," Maples said.

Boyd smiled at him, and went to the river to wash his plate and fork.

One by one the men did as well.

Some of them undressed and took baths in the river. Others simply washed their hands and faces in the water. A couple of others spread out their bedrolls and tried to go to sleep early.

At the river, Sullivan walked over to Boyd.

"Did ya think anybody was watchin' us today, maybe following us?"

"Naw, and I saw no sign of Indians anywhere. I don't think any know we are out here in the open."

"I hope you're right. These extra horses we are trailin' sure do make us a nice target. Hope none of them ever see us."

"Yeah, me too."

Sullivan walked up the river a little way. He took off his clothes and his boots. Then he waded out in the water and sat down. He laid back so that only his head was dry. Then he sat up, bent over and submerged his head. In a few minutes, he got out of the water. He sat down on a large flat rock. It was still very warm, even though it was late in the day, almost dark. When he had dried off some, he put his clothes and boots back on.

William Boyd came walking over to Sullivan.

"How ya want'a play it this time?" Boyd asked.

"I have no idea. Depends on how things look when we get there, I guess. We won't know till we get a look-see. Don't know nothin' about who is with him. We'll have to sneak in, me and you, and get a good look at the situation. Then too, we don't know what time of day or night we'll be gettin' there. That will determine a lot, I guess."

"Yeah. Hope he ain't well guarded."

"Me too."

"Time will tell," Boyd said.

"You better get some rest. It's been a hard day."

"What about you? You had the same day."

"Yep, but I don't sleep much. I'll be keeping alert a while, and I'll change the guards."

"All right," Boyd replied. "If ya hear somethin' let me know."

Chapter Forty-eight

Sullivan and Boyd crawled along a small rise just to the right of the trail leading to the cabin and about one hundred yards away from it. They were well hidden by small trees and bushes. They had a good view of the cabin. There were five horses in the corral off to the right of the barn which was on the left side of the cabin and thirty yards from it. There was a small stream of smoke rising from the chimney. They did not see any men walking around outside. They all were inside it seemed.

The other Rangers were holding all of the mules and the horses, theirs and those from the raiders, back down the trail about fifty to sixty yards away. They were up the side of the mountain in the woods in case someone came along. They were supposed to stay there unless Boyd came after them or unless they heard shooting. If they heard any shots at all, they were to come forward with all speed, leaving the mules and the raiders horses tied to trees.

Sullivan and Boyd kept lying there, trying to decide what to do.

It was already getting dark. Someone lit a lantern in the cabin. Then there was more light from another lantern Sullivan and Boyd assumed.

"What ya think?" Sullivan asked Boyd.

"I think it's getting dark real quick. Once the sun dropped behind the mountains, it don't take long."

"Yeah. I don't want to go in there shootin' in the dark. We might start shootin' each other by accident."

"We bout a half a day too late."

"I agree. Why don't we hit'em at sunrise before they get their bearings?"

"I think that's our best option."

"William, sneak back down there to the Boys and tell them what we'll do. They need to get some sleep. But at least one needs to be awake at all times. Tell'em we'll come get'em well before first light."

Boyd crawled away, headed for the other Rangers.

Sullivan lay there watching the cabin.

Suddenly he saw a flash of light. Someone opened the door and came outside.

It looked like it could be Jack Stalker. It was hard to see, but it was a large man with a dark beard and hair, no hat, dark clothing.

He stepped out off the small porch, and went around the right side of the cabin. He disappeared.

There must be an outhouse back there Sullivan thought.

He waited and watched, but it was getting darker, darker, darker.

Sullivan was wishing he had his Winchester with him, but it was now too dark for sure.

He could not be certain it was Stalker anyway. He did not want to shoot the wrong man and have Stalker get away. He had already shot the wrong man once. He did not want any more of that.

After ten minutes, the man came back, a dark shadow moving along beside the house. He turned the corner, stepped up on the porch, and there was the flash of light again as the man entered the cabin.

Fifteen minutes later, Boyd crawled up beside Sullivan again.

Sullivan turned toward him and spoke in a low voice.

"Guess what I saw."

"What?"

"I said guess."

"A mama bear with cubs."

"I think I saw Stalker goin' to the crapper. It looked a lot like him, but hard to tell in the dark."

"I wish you had your Winchester with you."

"I thought of that, but too dark. Couldn't be sure. I would have been afraid if it weren't him, he would get out the back door, if there is one, and be gone."

"Good thinkin'."

"Well, I guess we'll just stay here and wait till morning. Be a long night."

"Long one."

Sullivan and Boyd talked for a couple of hours. Then Boyd began yawning. Sullivan looked over at him.

"I think it's gettin' past yore bedtime."

"My . . . . ahhhhh, goodness. I think so too."

"Get some sleep. I'll wake you up later. One of us got to be awake long before dawn."

"Wake me, and I'll take the watch till near dawn," Boyd said.

"Good."

Boyd rolled over on his side. He folded his hat over and used it for a pillow. It was not much of a pillow, but then it was not much of a hat either.

Sullivan kept watching the cabin. Now and then, someone would come outside. He would see the flash of light at the door, but that is about all he could see. He could see a person moving, but could not tell who it was. It looked like some of them went to the outhouse. One man must have gone to check on their horses. Sullivan could see some movement there.

Around two o'clock, Boyd woke up, rolled over, and spoke to Sullivan.

"Anything goin' on down there?"

"Naw. Quiet as a church mouse."

"Pretty quiet. You get some sleep. I got it now."

Sullivan was lying on his stomach. He put his head down on his folded arms and drifted away.

Chapter Forty-nine

When Sullivan and Boyd went back to get the Rangers, they found them up and ready. They were standing by their horses, ready to go, but unsure if they would ride in or not.

"We'll leave the horse here," Sullivan said. "We'll go in on foot. Spread out when we get there on both sides of that cabin. Some of ya can take cover in that barn. William will be with you over there. Some of you come with me to the right side. It'll be light soon. If they ain't up, we'll wake'em up. No lights in the

cabin just now, but could be by the time we get there. Bring yore rifles with ya. You gonna need'em. All right, let's go."

Sullivan led the Rangers down out of the trees and onto the trail that led to the cabin. By that time, the sky was turning gray. The light was shining up over the eastern mountains and quickly spreading westward.

They saw there was a light in the cabin. The raiders were already up.

The cabin door opened.

"Down," Sullivan whispered.

They watched a man as he stepped out of the cabin and onto the porch. He walked to the right side of the cabin, tuned left, and headed for the outhouse.

Sullivan signaled for the men to raise up and follow him.

They hurried along the trail. As they approached the cabin, Sullivan pointed at the barn. Boyd and several of the Rangers headed that way. Then he pointed for the others to go to the right. They took cover behind an old wagon that looked like it had not been moved in years, but it was good to hide behind anyway.

Sullivan looked around, making sure there were no other raiders outside. Then he called out to the men inside the cabin.

"You in the cabin! Come out and meet yore maker or stay in there and meet yore daddy the Devil! Either way you about to die!"

There was silence for a moment. Then suddenly . . . .

Bang!

Bang!

Bang!

Pow!

Pow!

Bang!

A hail of bullets came roaring out of the cabin!

The Rangers began firing back!

Bang!

Bang!

Bang!

Bang!

Sullivan did not want Stalker to escape, so he ran toward the back of the cabin!

There was that man in the outhouse.

Sullivan stood half way between the cabin and the outhouse.

He pointed his Winchester at the old almost falling in structure.

Bang!

Bang!

Bang!

The half rotten door almost fell off. There was no movement inside. Sullivan walked over to the door and kicked it. It fell the rest of the way off. He looked inside. The man in there was not Stalker. There was blood and wood chips everywhere.

Sullivan whirled around and looked at the back of the cabin. There was a door. He decided to wait there and see what happened. He was not needed out front where a small war was taking place.

Bang!

Bang!

Bang!

Bang!

Bang!

Bang!

The two groups of Rangers out front were filling the cabin with lead!

And the raiders were throwing plenty of it outside with rifles and pistols!

Bang!

Bang!

Pow!

Bang!

Pow!

Bang!

Boyd decided that could go on all day or until someone ran out of ammo. He figured they had plenty inside, and would not run out any time soon.

He ran to the front of the cabin, and stood by the window on the left side of the door! He waited there a moment, then looked in the window and shot with his pistol the man who had been shooting out of it!

Pow!

Suddenly the back door swung open!

Sullivan pointed his rifle at the man who came rushing out!

The man stopped suddenly, surprised to see someone waiting on him!

"You Jack Stalker?"

"Yeah. What of it?"

"Drop yore pistol, Mister Jack Stalker."

Stalker let go of his pistol and it fell to the ground. He slowly raised his hands in the air, as Sullivan signaled with his rifle for him to do so.

"You believe in God, Mister Jack Stalker?"

"No. I don't. So what? You a preacher of some kind?"

"You believe in the Devil?"

"I don't believe in him or nothing."

"Well, you will soon because you're going to meet him. I'm not a preacher, but I am the undertaker."

Bang!

Jack the beast Stalker fell to the ground. He had a bloody hole right in the middle of his forehead. He lay on the ground in a crumbled mess.

There was still firing going on out front!

Bang!

Pow!

Bang!

Sullivan walked to the door of the cabin. He stepped inside and saw two men firing out windows they were kneeling before and one man lying on the floor.

Sullivan whistled as loud as he could!

Ssszzzzzzzzzeeeee!

The two startled men turned around and saw him, the last person they would ever see.

Bang!

Bang!

They rolled over on the floor.

There was silence now. It was all over.

Chapter Fifty

"There's two of'em out back. One is Stalker. He ain't no beast no more. The other'ern is in the crapper, what's left of'im. Bring them two in here. Then set this place on fire. Saves digging a grave for them which they don't deserve. Burn that barn too. These Boys gonna get a taste of what their eternity is goin' to be.

"Bailey, you and Dunken go get the horses."

While the men set out to accomplish their tasks, Sullivan

walked off by himself. He wanted to get his mind together a little after the intense period he and the Rangers had been through.

In a few minutes, Boyd walked over to him.

"What-cha thinking about so deeply?" Boyd asked.

"I'm thinkin' I'm glad this is over."

"Me too, of course."

"The Boys did a really good job, didn't they."

"Yes, they did," Boyd replied. "And you weren't half bad yourself."

"All in a day of work I reckon."

"What now?"

Sullivan turned around and looked at the cabin as the flames were just beginning to take hold of it. Smoke came billowing out of the doors and windows.

"Well, if we wanted to rest a day and sleep inside tonight, I just burned down our accommodations."

"Weren't but three beds in there no how," Boyd replied.

"Yeah, I'd sooner be on the ground staying awake most of the night than being on a hard floor."

"Me too."

"Soon as that barn is on fire and the horses get here, let's head out. We got a long way home."

"Sure."

Boyd walked off toward the barn.

Sullivan spit on the ground, thinking another job done.

Twenty minutes later, they were heading down the trail

out of the mountains. Sullivan was hoping they would never see the Quitman Mountains again. He looked over at Boyd.

"The Quitman Mountains. I quit."

"What?" Boyd asked, a little startled.

"Quitman Mountains. I quit these mountains, as in never coming here again. I hope."

"Oh, yeah. Me too."

Three days later, they were in El Paso. The desk man at the hotel called out to Sullivan,

"Mister Texas Ranger head man, I got a note here for you. It's from the commander at Fort Bliss. Want me to tell you what it says. I already read it twice."

"You said it's my note?" Sullivan asked, as he walked over to the counter.

"Yes, Sir, it is. From the commander at Fort Bliss, and he said . . . ."

"Thanks," Sulivan said, as he snatched the note from the man's hand.

He walked in the dining room and sat down at the table.

"What will it be, Sugar?" the waitress asked, with a big smile.

"Coffee. Just coffee."

"You sure?"

"Sure, I'm sure."

As she walked away, Sullivan took the piece of paper out of the envelope. He unfolded it and read the words.

Captain Sullivan, we have received reports of Comanche raids out to the east. Several ranches have been hit hard. There are no survivors. Some females may have been taken captive. I am taking a detachment out. Please come join us as soon as you return. We will not be hard to find. We will leave messages for you about where we are going.

Yours, Colonel Anthony Kicklighter

U S Army

Fort Bliss

"Here's your coffee, Sugar."

"Thanks," he said, without looking up.

Sullivan read the note again. It was just what he wanted, he thought.

He sat there for a while, slowly drinking the coffee. It was not very good. Had been left over from early that morning. But it was coffee. And it was what he needed.

Boyd looked in the dining room and saw him. Sullivan waved him over to his table. Boyd came in and sat down. The waitress suddenly appeared.

"What will it be, Sugar?"

"I'll have what he's drinkin'."

"Coffee, then?"

"Please."

"Read this," Sullivan said, as he handed the note to Boyd.

"Ummmmm."

"More trouble," Sullivan said.

"Looks like it."

"When are we leaving?"

"You and the Boys are leaving as soon as you can."

"What about you?"

"Here's your coffee, Sugar."

"I'm leaving as soon as I can."

"I don't get it."

"William, you need some experience being the leader. You will be a captain some day. This will be good training for you."

"Where you goin'?"

"I'm goin' east too, but I'm goin' all the way to Austin. I put a letter in the mail already asking for a one month leave. It'll beat me there. I'm goin' to see my darlin' lovin' wife. You boys be careful. And good luck to ya."

Toombs Sullivan got up and left the dining room.

"I'll pay for the coffee," Boyd said, as he watched Sullivan head for the stairs.

The End